Aliens on a Mission
The hidden forces.

Michael Peckmann & Rebecca Rosen

A story of trance music

Aliens on a Mission - The hidden forces.

Michael Peckmann & Rebecca Rosen

Published by
#EDM Publications
ISBN 978-0-692-76578-4
Copyright © 2017
All Rights Reserved
Art of Doing Publishing Inc.
2401 NE 200 Street, Miami, FL 33180 USA
www.edmpub.com

Cover design by Stephano Loyo

Published by #EDM Publications
Art of Doing Publishing Inc.
2401 NE 200 Street, Miami, FL 33180
Printed USA – 2017
First Edition

Copyrights Music:

Chapters

<u>Acknowledgements</u>

A **fictional story** inspired by real events, experienced by the authors of this book.
Thank you for your support.
Michael Peckmann & Rebecca Rosen
2017

The book Mr. Wagges dedicated, ask all electronic dance music lovers around the world, to dance for freedom.

The behind the scenes story gives a fascinating glimpse into the world of the burgeoning electronic dance music scene and its independent record labels.

I

Magic Trax

"Where is my love? Where is my love...?"

While the catchy electronic dance music sounds saturated the main room of Magic Studio, Mono peered out of his small window inside the recording cabin.
He seemed surprised to see that the studio now had a visitor.
Peter must have just come into the studio.
Eric Nouhan, the youngest of the studio owners, yelled over to Raul, "Let's call it quits for today, man."
Raul, the producers' assistant, gave a cheerful thumbs-up. He yelled back to Eric, "Do your shit, man! We have to tinker a bit more. We need to work on our arrangement!"
Tabitha, the star, was a beautiful young Girl, but she didn't possess it.
"We need a supporting voice, or we will stop right here," Raul sighed, throwing his headphones on the table in frustration.
"You're right, that's what I think."
Mono wore an air of confidence; he acted uncharacteristically nervous for this task.

The "Where is My Love?" project began as his first song production a few months ago. A problem existed; he had no Idea what he did doing. Mono materialized working with the help of a mysterious force.

Eric the French composer, Mono the German thinker, and Raul, the Portuguese professor all agreed that Tabitha seemed a perfect fit for the project. But ever since the production began, the crew had become increasingly frustrated. The twenty-year Dutch girl had no studio experience, and she evidently did not have the endurance to work long hours in the studio. It also appeared quite clear that she had no self-confidence as a singer. She naively accepted the project based on trust and love for Mono.

Mono's project emerged to be the first production in Amsterdam's Magic Studio.

The computer had crashed five times that day already. After the computer failed for the sixth time, Mono finally called an end to the day's work. His concentration had anyway faded ever since Peter's unexpected appearance.

Peter was an influential guy who acted as Amsterdam's self-appointed "Mr. Party", and a best friend with the principal shareholder of Magic Studio. A few years earlier, he had successfully launched the "Energy Hours" party in Zaandam, a lovely beach village close to Amsterdam. Since then, he had moved the Sunday parties to the Escape, the hottest venue in downtown Amsterdam.

Mono took stock of the situation. He knew through rumors that Peter, a guy in his mid-thirties, is upset because he wanted studio time in the new hot spot Studio in Amsterdam first. If rumors appeared right, Peter did a good job of masking his feelings.
Catching Mono's eye across the room, Peter smiled coolly and asked, "How is everything going?"
"Great, Peter, thanks for asking," returning the smile.
Finally, after a little more small talk, Mono and Tabitha left the studio.

After Mono's exit, Peter turned to Eric and asked bluntly, "Why are you teaming up with Mono?"
Eric seemed surprised to hear this question.
He answered with his naturally calm voice. "We should all explore options outside our comfort zone. He has his moments. I like the project."
Harold the happy Dutch, another studio shareholder, had walked in unnoticed, just after Mono and Tabitha left. He overheard Eric and Peter's brief exchange and jumped into the conversation before Peter could say another word.
"Mono's project is a business for our new studio."
Peter, the Dutch spy, decided to keep quiet for the time being and changed the topic of the conversation.
"So, have any of you guys heard the new song from DJ Jean & Peran?"

In front of the studio, Mono and Tabitha shared a long kiss and parted ways after. Tabitha wanted to visit her uncle, so she hopped into a passing taxi. Mono seemed in need of some fresh air and decided to walk the rest of the way back to his house. Walking briskly along the Rokin, one of the city's pretty main roads, he nearly ran right into his friend Daniel, the owner of Pantharei Television, a production company on Prinsengracht, one of Amsterdam's famous water streets.

Both acted shivering from the freezing winter wind.
"Hey," Daniel greeted Mono through chattering teeth.
"What are you up to these days?"
"Daniel it is great to see you again."
"Man, come on, it's fucking cold. Let's get out of this wind and get a coffee at the Rasta place down the street. Let's exchange some ideas." Daniel agreed.

The coffee shop crowded, and the air gray from cigarette and pot smoke. Mono ordered two coffee verkehrt, Dutch-style milk coffee. They stripped down to T-shirts and settled into the small wooden chairs.
What have you been up to lately?
Daniel, the good looking Dutch, took a sip of his coffee.
"Well," I am producing a fashion show that will be here in Amsterdam soon.
"This sounds interesting," Mono scratching his chin thoughtfully.

Daniel could see the wheels turning in his head and waited for him to respond.

"Actually," Mono went on, "I just might have an attraction for your show. Right now, I'm working with a new young Dutch singer. She's eye-catching, and I think she'd probably fit in somewhere in your program."

"I will keep it in my mind, my friend."

"We need to discuss this further," Mono responded enthusiastically. Daniel promised to stop by his office later next week. "Let's have another coffee, Mono!"

"I really should get going," Mono stood up from his chair and dropped a few Guldens on the table. "The tab is on me."

"I have already paid; take your coins back."

"Thank you, call me later, please. That was fun to see you today."

"It was nice seeing you too Mono."

On the way home, Mono mentally prepared the evening's menu. He would do the cooking himself, like always. Cooking occurred as one of his particular pleasures, and his pace quickened from both the piercing cold wind and the motivation to hit the kitchen. In less than fifteen minutes, he arrived at his house, right in front of the Paradiso, where the Stones once played a gig. Located southwest of the central district of Amsterdam, his house seemed in walking distance from nearly every cool entertainment location in town. Mono fell in love at first sight with Amsterdam in the autumn of 1986, when he visited for the first time.

Mono slid the key in the front door when Olga the smart Dutch, the company manager, opened a side door of the house and began to shout. Mono recognized Dance 2 Trance - "¿Where Is Dag?" continued pounding in the office.
"Jo and I have been waiting for you! I spoke with Magic over an hour ago, and they said that you had already left."
Mono chuckled at the lack of privacy in his affairs.
"Calm down, Olga," he said lightly, "what so important appeared? I'm right here, so just relax!"
"Yeah, okay," "but I knew if I didn't catch you now, you would run straight up to your apartment."
"You're right." "I am just about to cook dinner. Is that okay with you?" Mono asked.

From the inside of the office, Mono could hear Jo screaming, "It's Tabitha on the phone!"
Mono yelled back, "Tell her I will call her back in a few minutes."
Olga had worked for RW Records since day one; instead of heading straight to his place, Mono walked with Olga into his office so she could explain her anxiety.
"Look," she immediately began, "we are getting invoices from FedEx for shipments to Australia, and the weird part about it is that the invoices appear paid."
Jo the Dutch student, the distribution manager, piped in from his corner. "Maybe it's somebody else shipping goods in our company's name?" Joe had just recently begun working for RW Records.
Mono nodded and thought for about five seconds, before delivering his instructions.
"Olga, you check it out, okay? And please," Mono begged, "leave me in peace for the rest of the day. Ras Karby is visiting us tomorrow, and he demands my attention."
Mono said his goodbyes and ran out the door.
"Wow, Jo," Olga remarked, "Mono is fucking stressed out!"
Jo smirked.
"Olga," Jo said slyly, "doesn't forget Tabitha is only twenty years old. You can be sure she demands a hell of a lot of attention."
"You know what, Jo? I think you are just jealous because you wish you could be with Tabitha too."

Mono appeared unwinding under a hot shower when he heard the phone ringing. He stuck his wet hands outside of the shower and tried to grab the cordless phone. After a few slippery misses, he brought the handset to his soapy ear and heard Tabitha on the other end of the line. "Yeah, babe, get over." "But why don't you just take a cab to my house and let me finish my shower? As soon as I am ready, I will cook us a wonderful dinner, I promise."
Mono laughed about her next question.
"Yes, babe, we can listen to your song, too. Okay, let me go. Hurry up, and I will see you very soon."

Like clockwork, Mono walked into the kitchen, opened up the refrigerator, and took a quick inventory.
Jans, his housekeeper, did the shopping and made sure that there always existed enough food in the house. Janse, the Dutch mom, happened to be the angel of his house. She had worked for him since he arrived in Amsterdam from Ibiza in the fall of 1993.
Mono looked back and forth between his watch and the food and decided on a menu of chicken filets with cognac gravy. There wasn't enough time for an elaborate dinner.
The clock read 8:30 PM.
While he took the chicken fillets from the refrigerator, he felt a hand tightly grab his ass.
Tabitha had arrived.

"Wait, babe," he said, turning around with a grin. "We're going to eat in 25 minutes, okay? But after our dinner, I promise, I am open for an adventure."
Both exchanged a lustful glance, and he stuck his head back into the refrigerator.
While he finished cooking, Tabitha never stopped talking. She had an unusual pet name for Mono, and she repeated it in every other sentence – Mies. In German, it appeared to be the word for lousy, but she didn't know that, and he didn't have the heart to tell her. Tabitha, Mono's muse, emerged to be a simple person, lovely and honest.
Mono had spotted her for the first time in Zandvoort on a sunny beach day, 20 miles outside of the city. Few hours' later coincidence appeared to happen both met for the second time that day at the Richter nightclub in downtown Amsterdam.

The dinner occurred to be delicious, and he acted proud of his handiwork. They savored the end of a fine bottle of wine until Tabitha stood up and began to make the table.
"Leave the plates here," he crooned. "Janse is coming tomorrow morning, and you know how much she loves to clean."
After a small whine of protest, Tabitha conceded and left the plates on the table. She hated for people to wait on her.

One minute later, the incident seemed forgotten.
Tabitha switched on the stereo; Jam & Spoon–
featuring Plavka - "Right in the Night" occurred
hitting in the room.
She jumped on his knees, deftly pulling his shirt over
his head. She quickly opened his jeans. He said
something, but her eager lips covered his mouth. He
already could feel the heat coming from between her
legs. She managed, as always, to get her first orgasm
by pressing her pussy hard against his right thigh.

Mono had to be at the airport at 9 AM to pick up Ras,
the famous Jamaican. Mono looked at his watch and
saw that it appeared to be already ten minutes after
nine. He still had three more miles before he would
be at the terminal.
Looking up at the signs, he laughed at the airport's
silly different Dutch name -"Schipol." And
luchthaven, the Dutch word for an airport, seemed
just as funny for a foreigner.
To release a little stress, he thought for a second
about last night's hot sex with Tabitha. But just as the
corners of his mouth moved curling upwards, he
stayed already nearby the baggage claim.
Ras Karby sauntered out of the customs area with a
big smile on his face.
Mono greeted him with a friendly wave and walked
over to the waiting area.

"How ended up your flight, brother?" Mono asked as they exchanged a warm handshake.

"Pretty shitty," Ras griped. "And as you know, New York City is fucking cold on top of it."

"Ras, my man, and what the hell are you doing in Amsterdam? If you searched to get a little sun, you should've flown back home to Jamaica."

"Yeah, I know it, man? But here in Amsterdam, I can smoke some blazing pot, and that will for sure be enough to warm my soul."

Mono laughed.

He agreed completely with Ras's logic. But before Ras could get in another word, he grabbed his arm and rushed him out to the waiting car.

Less a half hour later, they appeared nearing Leidse Square. Mono finally changed the subject of the conversation from cheap sex to the evening's plans.

"OK, Ras," he explained, "I am going to drop you off at your hotel right now and give you a chance to relax and do your shit. Dinner will be at 8 PM at my house. Your manager will be our guest. Is that cool for you?"

Ras thought for a second and shook his head.

"Man, I will see Rashid in a little while because he is leaving town for few days, let us go to that fish restaurant instead. You know the one right by the Renaissance Hotel; we had dinner the last time I visited Amsterdam at the spot. I liked the red snapper. And I fucking loved our waitress."

Again, Mono acted laughing.

"OK, Ras, you got it. Give a hug to Rashid. I'll call and get a table. How about I pick you up at the hotel at 7:30? And one more thing, man. Take care, and welcome to Amsterdam."

"Thanks, brother; it's great to be here."

Mono stopped at a stop light and reminisced about his first encounter with Ras. The day he appeared together with his manager Rashid in front of his door, advising Mono to invest in a reggae music project.
"Shit!" Mono grumbled to himself. "There are never any parking spots in this city!"
On the streets surrounding his house, finding a free parking space occurred tougher than winning the lottery. After circling the block for the fourth time, he spotted an old friend out of the corner of his eye.
"Hey! Nakka D!" he screamed out the window, Nakka D, the funny Dutch turned around looking confused until his glance fell on Mono waving the left arm. Nakka D walked towards the car.
"How ya doing, man?"
"Pretty cool, pretty cool," Nakka answered.
"Please, brother, will you help me out for a second? I need you to take my car and just drive around for a little while. I've already got some people waiting for me in my office, and I can't find a goddamn parking spot anywhere."
Nakka D happily offered his assistance.
"I'm always here for you, brother," he said and slid into the front seat of the Jeep. "Just give me a call if you need your car back soon. Otherwise, I will just take the car home for a little while. I have a free spot right in front of my house."

"Pretty nice, man, thanks," Mono said. "Also, please say hi to your family for me."
On the short walk to his appointment, Mono laughed to himself, picturing the next thirty minutes of Nakka D's adventures. Nakka D would have filled up the Jeep with a bunch of hot chicks. Mono silently wished him well and went up the front stair to his office.

Roberto and Ernesto, the Italian friends from the "Zenith" party, had been waiting in the RW Record office for over half an hour already. B.B.E. - "Seven days and One Week" appeared streaming from the CD player in the room. They barely noticed the long wait, however, because they acted busy catching up with Olga and Jo. Mono entered the office.
"Hi, guys, what's up?" He yelled out.
Not waiting for an answer, he continued, "Roberto, Ernesto, tell me what's going on in Ibiza!"
Mono followed both since Roberto and Ernesto had thrown the first "Zenith" party at Bora Bora on the island.
They all exchanged a round of greetings, handshakes, and hugs. Roberto, who spoke better English, answered his question.
"Well, man, winter in Ibiza is quite different, as you know."
"Oh, I know it. That would explain why Ernesto over here is so pale," Mono teased.

"No, man," Ernesto piped in, with his thick Italian accent. "Last night I met two very nice and boiling Dutch girls. I couldn't catch even an hour of sleep before getting over to RW Records."
"Oh, poor Ernesto," Mono replied, in a sarcastic tone. "I feel sorry for you."
Roberto, Olga, and Jo all acted laughing.
The telephone rang, and Olga ran out to answer in another spot of the enormous room.
"OK, guys, let's get serious now," Mono said, sitting behind his desk before anyone else could crack another joke.
In seconds, the guys seated in the appointed chairs, and the meeting seemed underway, with Mono taking the lead. "RW Records decided to invest in the "Zenith" parties and release your debut mix album. We will split the profit after deduction of all costs if there is any. Is that fine with you guys?"
Roberto and Ernesto gave thumbs up.
"When you guys on planning to have the album in stores?"
"A few days before our summer closing party on the island would be good," Ernesto answered.
"RW Records would need your final track list at the end of June, to license all of the tracks in time. We will book Studio Time at Orange Records or SSR Studios, no later than the first day of August. Onno Klein will start to create the CD artwork at the beginning of the summer, based on your ideas." The album could go to print on August 15 with an open window of two weeks. What do you guys think?"
"Sure," Roberto answered, "This deadline is right for us. And we would love to have Onno on the team."

"Great," Mono said. "Will your party hosted by Pacha next summer?"
Right then, Olga walked back into the front and interrupted the conversation. "It's FedEx on the phone. Do you want to talk with them?"
"No, Olga, I already told you, I want you to handle that shit. Just let me know after everything is green."
She nodded quietly and left the group.
"Yes, we will be at Pacha for the summer. How many stores will sell our first CD?" Roberto asked.
Mono looked to Jo and repeated the question.
"Well, I would have to look in my files for the exact number. But with the Free Record shops alone, we have a lot and, most importantly, the prime locations around the Netherlands."
"That's cool," Ernesto said.
"Your guy's party is the best!" Mono exclaimed enthusiastically.
Almost as quickly as he had begun the meeting, Mono brought the discussion to a close.
"Look, friends, I hate to do this, but I have to leave in a minute. I have someone waiting for me at Magic Studio.
"No problem, man," Roberto assured him. "We had already invited Olga and Jo for lunch, and they are waiting for us."
"Cool. By the way, guys, what are DJ Carlos Diaz and Reche up to these days?"
Ernesto answered fast.
"They will mix our album; both are very busy guys now, even in the winter."
"Nice, give them our greetings," Mono said sincerely.
"Okay, boys, I'm out. See you all next time in Ibiza."

Mono hugged Ernesto and Roberto goodbye and turned to Olga for one last round of instructions. "Olga, I won't be back in the office today because I have to pick up Ras for dinner at 7:30. And please don't disturb me while I am working at Magic. I promise I will be at the office tomorrow morning at 9."

After the door had slammed shut, Ernesto commented to no one in particular, "That guy is like the wind."
"Yeah," Jo agreed. "But we do have a hell of a lot going on here at the moment."
Jo said more but noticed the office had a visitor. Tal, the Dutch scout, poked his head into the room.
"Hey, Tal," Olga chirped.
"Hi, Guys."
He got a round of smiles in return.
"We decided just about to go out for lunch," Olga explained. "Do you want to join us?"
"That sounds great, thanks! But please tell me, to where did Mono just run? I came by especially to show him Tabitha's new photos."
Olga told him to just leave the photos on the desk and that he would look at them the following morning.
"Come on, Tal, we are all starving."
"Yeah, but..."

By the time Tal reluctantly just left a note on the desk for Mono, the rest of the lunch party appeared already waiting on the sidewalk.

As Mono rushed down Weteringsschans, he caught a glimpse of the photographer walking up to his office steps.
"Oh, there goes Tal Frank," he thought out loud. "He must be having something new."
It seemed tempting, but he decided to let it wait until the next morning. Tal had been working for RW Records since day one.
Mono acted reminiscing about their earlier encounters when his stomach screamed out for food; he had forgotten to eat before he left the house for the airport. So, in the interest of time like always, he stopped and bought a hamburger from Mcee Donald as he always referred to the franchise.
Fifteen minutes later he arrived at the studio, and he could already feel the grease rumbling in his gut. Walking up the path, Mono grimaced in pain. He looked up when Hartmut walked out the front door. Hartmut, the wealthy Dutch, occurred to be the biggest and senior shareholder of Magic Studio, and also an old friend of his from early Ibiza days. Mono smiled; because he remembered how Hartmut had once been a notorious lady-killer, always showing off with his 1966 Cadillac.
"Hi," Hartmut returned the smile. "How are you?"

"I'm fine, thanks. What about you?"
"Oh," Hartmut moaned, "I am in a hurry as always.
Raul is already waiting in the studio for you."
He said nothing more and Hartmut rushed down the
path.

The first thing Mono saw upon walking into the
studio appeared Raul's face behind the small cabin
window, his brow wrinkled in concentration.
Mono nodded hello and directly commenced with his
recording studio ritual. First he prepared a coffee
with two sugars and heavy cream, next he poured a
glass of water, and finally, he sat down at the mixing
board to listen to the previous day's recordings.
He only needed to hear seconds of the track before
noticing Raul's changes to the original recording.
Mono acted upset.
 "Come on man," he snapped at Raul "you know how
much I hate this shit! Why are you playing around
with the track on your own? Our crew works together,
or we don't work at all. Am I clear?"
Raul shrank back and promised it wouldn't happen
again. But he appeared not particularly offended by
the outburst. Raul knew Mono seemed sure of his
work qualities and wouldn't stay angry for more than
five minutes. These eruptions occurred just part and
parcel of a harsh workplace persona.
Mono stubbornly refused to listen to the rest of the
corrupted recording.

"Hey, Raul," he asked distractedly, "what's up with Eric?"
"Oh yeah, he won't be here before 8 PM."
"Well brother, we will work alone for today because I have to leave at 6. By the way, isn't our new vocalist coming in today?"
"Yeah, she should be here any minute."
"Tell me a little bit about this chick before she gets here."
"Just listen to a sample of her voice. She sings in a rock band."
Raul popped in a tape, and they listened for a few seconds, nodding their heads to the rock rhythm.
"Wow," Mono commented, apparently impressed. "That's not a bad voice at all."

A half hour later, Mono drank his second coffee when Mandy exploded into the studio, loudly apologizing for her tardiness. The blonde, twenty-ish rock singer had a large presence for her tiny five-foot stature. Mono threw a questioning glance in Raul's direction, and Raul looked back with a shrug of his shoulders. Raul turned his attention to taming this brash young girl.
"Please, Mandy!" "First you are going to have to quiet down a little, and then we are going to try and get some work done here."

Seeing the grave look on both guys' faces, Mandy continued immediately silent. She looked at them apologetically and asked in a small voice, "Where are my lyrics?"

Mono had a smile on his face, and Raul appeared already behind the mixing board. The incident seemed forgotten, and they acted ready to get down to work.

"Look," Mono explained, "This project is different, so don't expect anything more than the studio work."

"As long as I get paid," Mandy replied, "it is fine with me. It's funny, you know, I know Phil Aroza, the guy who wrote this song's lyrics."

"Wow," Mono replied, "that's interesting. Phil is a good friend of ours."

"Anyway," he went on, concluding the small talk like always, "let's get to work."

The guys needed to record her vocals few times only until both he and Raul acted satisfied with the results. Mandy performed proving herself a great singer as well as a professional in the studio. She left the studio sooner than she had anticipated happy.

Raul rewound the tapes, and they listened carefully with a look of intense concentration on the faces.

"OK, Raul, I think we can go for it, but confirm with Eric when he is in."

Raul happened already busy with the next step. "And you know what? I can do the mastering tomorrow so that by the weekend…"

The sentence trailed off as Raul realized his mistake.

"Shit," Raul exclaimed, "it's not possible. Eric told me that his Macintosh HD is corrupt. But anyway, I will get a new one tomorrow in Hilversum."

"What time tomorrow?"
"Tomorrow morning."
"OK, I will be at the studio at 2 PM. Make sure you are on time and that Eric is also here." "You can count on me." Mono appeared satisfied and prepared for his exit. "Hold on a sec Mono; I will leave as well, need some fresh air.
Mono and Raul left the studio together.

II

Hot Weekend Amsterdam

Olga has been particularly giddy after her lunch with the guys. She liked Roberto, a little bit more than she seemed willing to admit openly. She happened still smiling to herself as she dove back into her work. But her happiness faded as the conversation with FedEx led down the same dead-end street. The company representative kept repeating the same damn thing.
"It is billed for a shipment to Sydney, Australia."
And Olga kept giving the same exasperated response.
"Look, sir, we have not made shipments to Australia since months!"
The guy on the other end of the telephone occurred to be nothing more than a robot, and finally, Olga slammed down the phone in frustration. She could not handle the situation anymore and decided to leave a note for Mono on his desk.
"FedEx thing still not clear."

L.S.G. - "Fontana" did beating from the sound system in the room.

"A fax from Bonzai Records is coming in and another from BMG Universal." Jo bellowed across the room.
"Olga, it's for you!"
Olga did not move, Jo picked up the faxes and walked over to her desk with a thick stack of papers.
"It's for you, the last licensing agreements for the "Hot Weekend Amsterdam" compilations."
Olga emerged panicking.
"That's not good oh my god. It will put our timeline in immense trouble."
"What's wrong Olga?"
"Bonzai Music can't license Aspiral - "Heavenly," to our territory."
"Let me have a look," Joe asked and checked the content of the documents. "We can license the vocal mix of "Heavenly," check it again."
Joe handed the papers back to Olga.
"Oh, cool," Olga sighed, sounding relieved for the first time all day. "Mono will be triumphal."
She left a series of bright yellow notes on his desk.
"Licensing records complete.
Did you talk to Onno and Tal Frank regarding our deadline?
We need a studio appointment for The Funky Fakirs."
Looking at the desk, Olga knew that Mono would go fucking crazy when he showed up at the office the next morning.
"Jo!" she shouted, "please don't forget to tell him that I won't be in the office until Monday afternoon."
"What? Olga, you can't do that!
We have way too much work in the office right now."
Olga appeared not happy about his comments, furious shaking her head.

"Oh, yes I can," Olga said firmly. "I told him two weeks ago that as soon as we had finished all of the licensing agreements for the records, I would take a long weekend off."
"Yeah, sure, Olga, but this isn't fair, Ras is in town."
"Shut up, Jo! Just tell him I will be back on Monday." The door slammed, cutting off Jo's unenthused "good-bye." Jam & Spoon Mix – "The Age of Love" going loud from the office sound system in the room.

"Harold," Hartmut asked, "tell me honestly, what do you think about my buddy Mono?"
Harold and Hartmut appeared sitting across from each other at the conference table at Magic Studio. Harold thought carefully about the question before answering.
"Well," "I see his project, recommended by the Van der Made family. And, most importantly, he is paying our bills."
"Yeah, you're right." "But, the fact will always remain that Mono is a German."
"Yeah, I know."
The conversation stopped as Raul entered the room. He immediately picked up on a strange feeling in the air. Taking note of the questioning look on Raul's face, Hartmut quickly asked, "Raul, when will you be at Macintosh in Hilversum?"
"By tomorrow morning,"

"That's great, Raul. Our equipment will be complete by tomorrow afternoon. And Mono will finally be able to finish Tabitha's song."
Raul remained sure that something did going on between Harold and Hartmut, but he could not figure out what. Instead, he disappeared into the recording cabin and immersed himself in the music.

"Listen, babe" Mono talking with Tabitha on the phone, "you have to be at the studio at 2 PM tomorrow. We finished your song and hopefully by Monday the mastering will be done."
"Oh, Mies, you make me happier each day of the week. I love you."
"I hope so," But Tabitha, I can't see you tonight because I will be at dinner with Ras."
"Why not?" she whined, "I can come out with you guys."
"No, Tabitha."
"Why? Are you going to pick up girls with him?"
"Come on, babe, stop with these stupid questions. Ras is only in Amsterdam for twenty-four hours, and we need to talk business."
"Okay, fine," she huffed, "but I will wait for you at your house."
"Do whatever you want, Tabitha, you are always welcome, and you know that."

The clock already read 7:05 am. Mono had less than thirty minutes to pick up Ras, but it seemed more than enough time. Rasta stayed at the American, his favorite hotel just across Leidse square.

Ras appeared waiting in the hotel lobby, but his mind wandered elsewhere. Ras's thoughts acted back to a dream he had one night.
In the dream, he seemed to ride on the back of a motorbike, cruising down a beach road in Jamaica.
All of a sudden, the bike stopped, and Ras jumped off. On the side of the road, Ras saw a guy standing with his face hidden by shadows. The guy said to Ras, "Hey, man! Do you know who arrived driving that bike with you?"
Ras immediately turned around, but he couldn't see anything except dust clouds as the bike sped away. Suddenly, the driver stopped the motorcycle and turned his head to look back at Ras. The biker said only one thing.
"Go to Amsterdam."
Ras went crazy and began to scream, "Man, it's Bob! Look, it's Bob!"
The guy standing next to him nodded and kept repeating, "That's right, man, it's Bob Marley."

"Are you daydreaming or what?"
"Oh, sorry, I traveled thousands of miles away with
my thoughts."
"Come on," sizing his shoulder, "our taxi is waiting.
And I have a surprise for you."
"What is it, man? Oh, man, tell me you will be getting
us a little bit of special service tonight."
Ras winked and flashed him a sleazy grin.
"Well, kind of," he answered slowly, ducking into the
back seat of the taxi.
"Tell me more; I'm totally curious now."
"Be patient, brother, you will see soon enough. And
close your door, man, it's fucking cold here."
He leaned forward to give their driver instructions to
the Renaissance Hotel.
Once the car emerged moving, he relaxed in the seat
and continued the conversation with Ras.
"I will be soonish in Los Angeles," "and thank god the
weather is not nearly as shitty over there. What about
you Ras, what are your plans?"
Without thinking, he quickly replied, "Now that you
mention it, I'm coming with you to LA."
But then he slowed down and said, "Yeah, I wish. But
seriously, I have to stay in freezing New York City.
I'm writing a play for Broadway, and I have to finish
it in ten days."
The car screeched to a halt, and the driver looked
back expectantly.
"Look, we're already here. Let me pay the dude."
"No way," "you're my guest tonight."
"Sounds good to me man."

"I knew it all along, Ras. It happened to be never about the red snapper for you. It seemed all about the waitress, right?"

"Oh man, you knew from the very beginning. You've made me so happy with your special services. I've never in my life had a fucking red snapper and "a special" at the same time.

Amsterdam is sensational. That is fucking great. Know what, man? If you want, you can have the worldwide rights for "Jah Rastaman" for $15,000 bucks advance."

"That's very cool; Ras, but you know what? I'm not Rockefeller. To combine a house sound with your number is just an idea to mix cultures. I don't have the money to spend so much up front just for an idea. Do you get me? And what existed with your publisher Rasta Music? Past many years since this song hit the charts."

"Oh man," "I can't do it for any less. It developed as a number one song, recorded at the legendary Tough Gong studio."

""Yeah, but a long time ago in Jamaica," He laughed. "And no company in the whole fucking world would pay that kind of money in advance; it's a high-risk investment. Look, Ras, let me see how everything is in a couple of months and I will get back to you."

"OK, fine. Now, what are we doing for the rest of the night?"

"Tabitha is waiting for us at the house, but I guess we should first go around the corner and smoke a joint. What do you think?"

"Let's do it."

Amsterdam is hands-down the best city in the world for smoking pot. There is never any hassle with insane laws, and the selection of weed is always first-class.

Both he and Ras appeared smoking the weed "pure" and Mono seemed stoned as hell. Ras looked not quite so bad.

Finally, after a half-hour of laughing at all stupid jokes, Mono calmed down and told Ras it's time to leave.

Ras begged him to stay for just another hour.

"I am invited to pick up the waitress," he explained.

"Okay, man, I will stay for you. But I think that your ass came to Amsterdam only for the waitress and not for our business at all. I guess this means I won't see you again tomorrow morning?"

"Nope," said Ras, "the girl should drop me off at the airport."

"Oh man, when did you make all of these arrangements?"

"Oh, you know I'm a Rasta Man."

The taxi stopped right in front of Weteringsschans 37. Somehow Mono managed to pay the driver quickly, but when he swayed the three levels to the front door; he just could not find the doorknob. The best he could do begin to laugh at his stupidity. So he did for more than a minute.

Finally, he managed to open the door and turned on the light. His house presented 116 years of history and had typical Amsterdam stairs, very tiny and steep. For a high man, it appeared to be a major obstacle. He stumbled up to his second-floor bedroom, using a wall for support and continued walking. His bedroom seemed to be enormous, existed one big room separated into three areas, a dining room, a sleeping chamber, and a bathroom. The whole house had been the concept of the great Dutch artist Wim Peters. "Hallo Mies! Hallo Mies!"

Mono could hear Tabitha screaming his pet name. He had completely forgotten that she would be waiting in the bedroom. Mono walked in and flipped on the light. Symphony of Love III - "The Angels Sing" – Love Tribal Dub appeared kicking from the sound system in the room.

"Hey babe, what's up?"

And there she appeared, lying on his bed, decked out in her favorite sexy lingerie. Her skin looked especially soft in the room's yellow light.

"Come on, get me," "I can't wait anymore. Look how wet I am. I've already made myself cum two times." She squeezed her tits and opened her well-formed long legs. Mono felt a magnetism pull his head towards her cleanly shaven pussy. "Harder!" Tabitha screamed, but soon she could not say another word; she occurred in the throes of a major orgasm.

"Oh no," Mono moaned, "What the hell is that noise?"

There happened to be a bass drum pounding in his head. The reality of the morning quickly woke him up.

He rolled over and whispered, "It's 8 AM, Tabitha, and I have to go to work."

She mumbled something that sounded like "okay."

The shower seemed thoroughly refreshing for him.

He stayed completely in love with his bathroom.

Nobody could have negative thoughts in such a gorgeous bathroom, even after a rough night in Amsterdam.

He appeared still squeezing the water from his long hair when he walked into the third-floor kitchen.

Janse arrived already there, patiently waiting for the orders.

"Morning, Janse."

Janse returned the morning greeting in her particular manner that he loved so much.

"You are too skinny,"

"Oh, Janse, you are my mom."

"I know that," she smiled.

"But please," "make two eggs for me. I am in a big hurry this morning."

"You are always in a hurry. How do you want your eggs?"

"Over easy."

Janse quickly cracked two eggs into the pan and brought out some warm bread.

"You need to take your time for breakfast," she said. "Now, sit down, or I really will get angry with you. What is with Tabitha? She doesn't want to eat breakfast?"
"No, not now, she continued still sleeping."
"Mono," she said in a disapproving tone, "this girl is not right for you."
"Come on, Janse, that's none of your business."
Janse shook her head and brought the plate to the table.
He dove into the eggs, sopping up the bright yellow liquid with a fresh piece of brown bread.

Mono leaned all the way back in his plush leather chair, thoroughly enjoying the silence in his office. But, looking down at his desk, he seemed to be immediately in the mood to go back to bed again. The desk covered in little yellow notes that Olga had written the day before.
He began sifting through the mess of papers and stopped when one particular note piqued his interest. He thought for a second and picked up the phone.
"Onno?"
"Yeah what's up Mono?"
"How are you doing?"
"I'm cool, what's up?"
"Listen, I just found a note from Olga here on my desk. We completed all of the licensing agreements for the records. So when can I see the artwork?"

"What about this afternoon?"
"No," Mono answered quickly, "that's not possible. I will be at Magic Studio all afternoon. Let's say 7 PM at my office? And, do me a favor, please. Can you call Tal? I want to have him around as well."
"No problem, man, I already told Tal to keep his schedule open."
"Great, see you at 7."
He could hear Onno the Dutch designer saying good-bye as he hung up the phone. His stress somewhat alleviated after talking to Onno, and Mono almost couldn't hide his excitement about the current positive situation. He knew he could count on both Onno and Tal. The artwork could be the thing.

Mono switched on the CD player and recognized the voice coming from the speakers and began singing with him together.
"Electrica Salsa, Baba baba - mmh mmh - aha aha — oh...." Listen to the magic words Hazam halum gelum daza Niaculum lulum sazaHasum halum gelum daza Niaculum lulum saza Don't have to ask you to get up You'll do it on your own****".

Flashbacks about his electronic dance music birth hit him instantly. Images appeared in his mind, Metropol, Vogue, Music Hall, Dorian Gray, Marilyn, Boccaccio, Omen, Space, Amnesia, Pacha, and KU. The times with Wagges the German Guru, getting inspired by "our force," partying, XTC, dreaming and making plans with friends, being happy and dancing to tunes of Bijan Blum, Sven Väth, DJ Dag, Jam El Mar and Mark Spoon. Carl Cox, Talla, Ulli Brenner, Andy Duex, Tom Wax, Rashid Nouri, Sherry Ansari, Ferno Madmud, Attilio Messina, Nicolas Vegas, Ralf Holl, Mete Bozkurt, Freak, Raphael Krickow, DJ Sidney, DJ Taucher, Dig, Tanith. Sasha. The Hypnotist, Seqeuntial, Koma, DJ Sakin, Torsten Stenzel, Marusha, Westbam, Dr. Motte, Mate, Galic, Jens Lissat, Michael Muenzing, Luca Anzilotti and Torsten Fenslau – RIP. Alfredo, Cesar De Melero, Pippi, Alex P, Brandon Block, Carlos, Siko, Colin Hudd and a lot more.

He appeared still leaning back in his chair, deep in a trance, when Mono caught a glimpse of Jo rushing into the office.
"Morning, Jo."
"Sorry, I am a bit late."
"Yeah, I can see that. The first time in a week I am here early in the morning, and everybody else is late! Where is Olga?"
"Olga is off until Monday afternoon."

"Oh, fuck, I forgot,"
"Is Ras coming to the office this morning?"
"No, Jo, he did leave at 8:30 this morning for New York. He only came for the day. Can you believe that he came all the way to Amsterdam for twenty-four hours, just for his dick?"
"What's that supposed to mean?" Jo asked.
Mono said nothing and only smiled.
"Another thing," "how many record stores do we have in the Netherlands in total?"
"We have around one thousand and growing by the month."
"And our music is in how many, do you have the number already?"
"The largest chain Free Record has one hundred stores alone."
"OK fine with me, that's amazing anyway!"
"Yeah," Jo said, "but we will get into stores all over the world."
"We will see," "But let's talk about the present for a minute. I told you that I am going to be in LA for a time, right?"
"Yeah, but when will you leave?"
"I think around January 8th or little earlier."
"Oh, nice, so that means we will both be in Amsterdam for New Year's?"
"Yeah, I guess so,"
"Listen, Jo," "I need you to arrange a studio appointment for The Funky Fakirs."
"Sure but where at Magic?"
"No, not there let's go for more space."
"Okay," Jo said, "that's fine with me. When should I make the appointment?"

"As soon as possible but you will have to deal with The Funky Fakirs on our own and no mistakes, okay?"
"No problem man."
But he seemed not yet finished with his instructions. "There is one more thing, Jo. I don't understand this whole FedEx story. But I know that something is wrong. Here on this invoice, it is written RW Distribution on top of our office address. But we are RW Records. I don't get it. And Olga couldn't clear it up on the telephone. Will you please drive down to FedEx and speak personally with them? Check with the tax number they have on file. Maybe you will be able to find out what the hell is going on."
"Okay, but it is going to have to wait until next week."
"Yeah, but next week we have already Christmas........You know what? Fuck it, Jo, do it at the beginning of the New Year. Just leave Olga a message on her desk, so she knows that you are handling the situation."
"You got it." Jo walked to his desk.
As the boss of RW Records, Mono sounded notoriously tough. He refused to settle for anything less than perfection and expected all employees to work with equal intensity. But with the licensing agreements out of the way, there happened to be little left to do before the end of the year, and he could not be so demanding. The sound of Globe - "Pulse" put Mono in a good mood.
Jo headed straight to the telephone, still feeling a little bit guilty for his tardiness. First, he would deal with The Funky Fakirs studio arrangements. He called Max, the London DJ, one-half of the artist duo.

"Hey, Max Jo here."

"Hi, Jo, what's going on?"

"First of all, Max, we have all the licensing agreements for the compilation records together. I emailed you the track list yesterday, and we should have all of the master recordings by the beginning of next week."

"Yeah, I know," he answered, "I already saw your mail."

"Great. We need to schedule the studio arrangements, and of course Mono would like to do it as soon as possible. Do you know Gino's Plan?"

"Sure I do. Gino's in New York City right now, and by Christmas, we will both be in London.

"Okay," Jo said slowly, flipping through his agenda. "I will make studio arrangements for January 10 at 6 pm. Confirm it with Gino please and let me knows if it is okay for both of you guys."

"Yeah, Jo, I'll talk to Gino. But for now, I am going to mark it down in on our schedule."

"Perfect Max and have a happy new year."

"For you as well Jo," Max responded.

With little left to do for the remainder of the afternoon, Jo kept himself busy organizing his desk. He decided to check in on the boss and found him leaning back in his chair, staring straight ahead and clearly deep in thought.

"Hey! Are you day dreaming?"

"Huh? Oh. No, Jo, I'm just checking my emails."
He dropped his gaze onto the computer screen and typed a few words to legitimize his claim. But the pensive look on his face remained, and after a few seconds, he looked up at Jo once again.
"You know what, Jo? I have a question."
"Go ahead."
He waited patiently, trying to imagine what his question would be. Jo could tell from the intensity in Mono's eyes that he would be making some interesting observations. Mono appeared silent and continued thinking to himself. Finally, he delivered the question. Robert Miles's - "Children" happened to be dreaming in the office.
"Jo, what do you think about Peter?"
"Which one you are talking about?"
"The "Energy Hours" Peter,"
"Oh, that Peter. You know, Olga worked for him for a while."
"Yes, I know that. But I want to hear your opinion about Peter."
"Well, Olga has told me some stories about things that happened while she worked for him. So I can't give you a right opinion today. You understand what I'm trying to say?"
"Of course, I get it."
Mono decided not to push any further, so he gave up on that line of questioning and changed the subject.
"By the way, Jo, what's the news about the studio for The Funky Fakirs?"
"We will rent the studio January 10, after 6 pm. But I'm still waiting for Max's final confirmation."

"Okay, that's fine with me. Those guys don't need me around anyway."
"Alright but now I have a question for you. What is JB doing? I haven't heard anything from him since he left the office a while ago."
"You aren't the only one. I saw JBs girlfriend Usha the other day. We spoke for a little while, but the conversation ended definitely kind of strange. Usha told me that she doesn't have any contact with JB anymore. You know what, though? I'm pretty glad as things are right now. What do you think?"
"Oh yeah, I totally agree. I just hope that the ID&T deal will happen."
"The connection is imperative for our plan. We are working on it. Alright, Jo, I am hungry, and I need a break. Let's go get some lunch."
"Fine, but who pays?"
"Who paid last time?" Mono countered, with a knowing grin.
"Okay, okay," Jo playfully grumbled. "You got me."

"Wow, Raul, you already have coffee ready for me. That's nice."
"Come on, Mono, I already know your little habits. You are a man who sticks to what he likes."
Mono smiled because Raul had hit it right on the nose. The thinker had always been a creature of habit and coffee happened to be one of his number one habits.

"You got me, Raul. So, what's up with the HD?"
"I picked it up in Hilversum. I already tried it, and it's
working fine. And by the way, Tabitha will be late.
She called a few minutes ago and said that there
seems to be something wrong with her Uncle Billy."
"Alright, let me hear your magic."
Raul turned on the music, and both listened to the
track. Mono acted apparently satisfied.
"Wow, man, without Mandy's voice, this would never
have worked. Tabitha just does not have enough
power to her voice."
At that exact moment, Tabitha walked into the studio
and caught the end of the conversation.
"What don't I have?"
Trapped, Mono could only reveal the truth. "You are
one of the hottest dancers in the world," Mono said,
"but you can't sing," He prepared for what he knew
should be coming next.
He grimaced and begged, "Please, Tabitha, don't
scream!"
Tabitha had finally calmed down. She sat down at the
head of the big table, where he and Raul appeared
still busy discussing the progress of the song.
"Raul," "what are your thoughts?"
"I think that we got what we asked for."
"Great, I agree. Tabitha, what about you? Do you
have any more thoughts about your song?"
"Well, actually," she answered slowly, "I can't hear
my voice anymore, only Mandy's."

"Babe, you don't have one," And before she could whine in protest; he added some comforting words. "But we all know that your voice is there, and you did an excellent job. We are all very proud of you. By the way, what's up with Billy?"

"Oh, they put my uncle in the hospital again. But he will be okay for now. It's a sad story, a sad story....." Tabitha's voice trailed off, and she looked out the window in silence.

Mono understood and left her alone in her thoughts and turned to Raul.

"Can you please burn a copy extra of the track for me? I want to pass it on to a friend, and maybe we can get the song on TV."

Tabitha immediately snapped out of her reverie.

"Mies, are you kidding? I don't believe it."

"No, I am not babe."

"Which channel and since when do you know it?" Raul also acted visibly excited.

"Let it be a surprise, Raul."

"Mies, you didn't tell me either!"

"I said maybe, Tabitha. Okay? And, please keep it confidential."

"Yeah, sure," Raul nodded.

"Tabitha, are you ready to go?"

"Yes, I am."

"Okay Raul, when can you drop off the master at my office?" Mono asked.

"By Monday morning would be easily possible."

Both stood up and said goodbyes nicely. As the lovers' walked hand in hand out the door, Mono turned back and yelled to Raul, "Oh yeah, and tell Eric I like his version very much."

Raul shouted back, "I told Eric that you would notice!"
"Of course, man, of course."

"Mies, what are we going to do on this late Friday afternoon?"
He looked at his watch and acted surprised to see it appeared already 6 PM.
"I guess we could visit Angela and Sanni," "Let me give them a call." He took his phone out of his briefcase and dialed the number.
Angela answered the phone and told him to wait a second.
"Angela Mono's on the phone!"
He could hear her muffled screaming. Finally, Sanni picked up on another extension.
"Hey, brother, what's up?"
Angela acted still fumbling with the phone as she hung up on her end. He waited until she seemed off the line and answered Sanni with another question.
"What are you doing, man?"
"Not much. Nakka D is here."
"Oh yeah? That's cool. Tabitha and I will come to your home. We should be there in a few minutes."
"OK, see you guys soon."

As soon as he and Tabitha had walked out of Magic Studios, Raul ran straight to the telephone. Raul heard a voice on the other end of the line; he immediately shouted, "Hartmut! It's Raul."
"Raul, what's up? You sound a little bit excited over there."
"Mono just left the studio."
"Oh! You guys finished with the song?"
"Yeah, but that's not why I'm calling. Before Mono left, he dropped a little info."
Hartmut's ears pricked up.
"What do you mean?"
"He will get the song played on a station!"
"Are you sure?"
"Well, he said maybe. But from what I have seen from Mono so far, it makes it possible."
"It sounds very exciting!"
Hartmut seemed quickly self-conscious of the excitement in his voice. He lowered his tone of voice and added nonchalantly, "Let me know if you hear any more about it."
Hartmut quickly changed the subject.
"Oh, Raul, I have meant to remind you. On Monday, Peter will start to record his new song in the studio."
"Oh yeah, that's right, I forgot about that."
"Did you tell anyone yet?"
"No, I didn't tell anyone of course. But why, Hartmut, is it a secret?"
"It's not a secret, but Peter specifically asked me to keep it under wraps."
Hartmut felt the need to end the conversation. He didn't want to talk about anything anymore.

"Listen, Raul," he said, "I have to get going. But do me a favor and leave Harold a note on his desk to call me as soon as he gets to the studio."

Hartmut hung up the phone, picked it right back up again, and dialed a new number.
"Peter? Hi, it's your buddy Hartmut here."
"Oh, hey Hartmut, I didn't expect to hear from you today. How are you doing? Is everything okay?"
"Yeah, Peter I'm fine, thanks. Listen, I'm in a hurry, but there is something you need to know."
Peter perked up just as Hartmut had when he first got the news.
"What do you mean?"
"He is telling people that he's going to get Tabitha performing "Where is My Love?" on TV."
"No way man, this Mono is bullshitting to keep you guys on track."
"Peter, I don't think so. From the way Raul just told me, he sounds rather dangerous. But Peter, the information just stays between us, okay?"
Peter didn't feel it necessary to answer this question. He and Hartmut had a personal confidence between each other.
"Do you know the channel and the date?"
"Not yet, but I should be aware pretty soon."

"Listen, Hartmut, please let me know as soon as you find out more about it." There emerged an awkward moment of silence. Finally, Peter found something to say.

"You guys are coming to my party at Escape on Sunday morning?"

"Yeah, Peter, for sure. Sunday morning "Energy Hours" at Escape is the best party in town. Nobody would miss it. Please put all of us on the list."

"Don't worry you guys are on our permanent guest list anyway."

Sanni, the Hungarian DJ, opened the door and found Mono and Tabitha with big smiles on both faces.

"Sanni, my friend," Mono greeted.

"Hi brother, Hi Tabitha, Please come in."

"Hi, Sanni," "Where is Angela?"

"Oh, she just left with Nakka D to buy some drinks. But they will be back any minute. Would you guys like to drink tea with me?"

Both accepted the offer in unison. "A tea would be nice, thanks."

The three of them moved into the kitchen, where Sanni put the kettle on the stove and took out two more cups. Without looking up from the counter, he began a little bit of small talk.

"What's up with the song?"

"This afternoon we finally finished," Mono answered excitedly. "I think we will get the song played on TV."

"Which station?"
"I promise you Sanni you will be the first to know, okay?"
"I am pretty sure that it will be worth the wait."
So, anyway," Mono continued, "You guys have any plans for the weekend?"
"Well, I thought we go to "Chemistry" on Saturday night. "After Energy Hours" on Sunday morning."
"It sounds fine with me. Babe, what do you think?" He looked over to Tabitha.
"Well, Mies, that sounds great to me too. But I have to buy some new clothes tomorrow."
Mono knew exactly the look that appeared playing across Sanni's face.
"Sanni, man, come on. Stop teasing."
"Okay, okay, I'm sorry," Sanni chuckled.
"Anyway, here, your tea seemed ready."
As Sanni handed out the steaming teacups, the front door opened, and Angela and Nakka D rushed into the room. They all exchanged the obligatory hugs and greetings.
"Brother?" "Are you getting any cute girls with my car?"
"Oh yeah, man, thanks," feigning a look of embarrassment.
"You know me, Nakka D continued. "But I promise, I will bring the car back tonight. I hope I'm not interrupting your plans."
"No, man, I don't have anything planned. Just don't forget, whenever you go home, I need you to drop Tabitha and me off at Leidse Square."
Nakka D nodded, and Sanni broke into the conversation. "Is it true that Ras appeared in town?"

"Yeah, he showed up here, but only for one day."
"Well, did you decide? Are we going to make a house remake of "Jah Rastaman"?"
"Actually, no, it's not possible right now because Ras is asking for too much money. But maybe we will work something out at the end of the summer."
Sanni asked Angela to bring him a can of Coke from the refrigerator, and he turned to the stereo.
"Listen to this song, guys. It's the new one from DJ Jean & Peran. The song is fresh, excellent."
"I like the sound a lot," listening carefully to the beats. "Both deserve huge success."
The three guys stood in a circle talking about dance music until he heard Tabitha talking, softly and from the corner of the room.
"I'm tired, Mies. Let's go home please."
"Wait just ten more minutes, Tabitha. Nakka D is rolling a joint for us. After the joint, I promise, we will leave. Nakka D, you are coming with us, right?"
As he blew out a puff of thick smoke, "I just changed my mind. I'm going to stay here."

Mono and Tabitha got the vehicle back from Nakka D and headed home. Jam & Spoon—Featuring Plavka - "Find Me" - Odyssey to Anyoona happened to be beating in the car. Right as the Jeep turned the corner, he remembered his appointment. "Tabitha, you know what? I forgot about my meeting with Onno and Tal! They have been waiting for me at the office since 7 PM! But you know what? If both are still there, Tal should have your new photos with him."

"Oh, Mies, do you think both are still there?"

"Yeah, I think so, at least if Jo is still in the office. Otherwise, they would have called me already. Oh fuck," he realized, looking down, "my phone is turned off!"

"Mies, look, there's a parking spot in front of your house."

"Whoa, babe, that's great. You're good! I'm not moving the car all weekend. And look in the office, there is still light. For sure they are all there. So, are you coming into the office to see your pictures?"

"No, not right now" she answered softly. "Can you bring them with you later? I forgot I need to walk to my uncle's house first to see how he's doing. He is back from the hospital I hope."

The door opened, and Mono made his usual grand entrance. The sound of Fly - "Multitudes of Sins" - Lovin in the Dark Mix played pounding in the office.

"Here he is!" Jo announced. "He's late, but I told you he would make it."

"Sorry, guys," he apologized. He walked over to Tal to give him the first hug.

"Tal, my friend, what's up?"

After the hug, Tal said nothing and quickly opened up the big black briefcase he had placed by his feet. He acted excitingly digging through the case until he plucked out a stack of photos.

"Look, here are the new pictures. Aren't they beautiful?"

"Tal please let me relax for a second. And Jo thanks for waiting for so long."

Jo acknowledged the apology with a nod.

"Just to let you know, on Monday I won't be in the office. I am going out to Hilversum to deliver the master. Raul just called he would drop the CD in my house on Sunday afternoon. See you on Tuesday."

"Oh, yeah, thanks."

And he took a deep breath, smiled at Tal and Onno, and seemed finally relaxed.

"Okay guys; let me see if you caught my angle."

Tal, Onno, all had their heads buried on the table, carefully examine the printed designs.

"Onno," Mono chirped, "this emerged fantastically! Tal, don't you agree?"

"Of course, appeared it to be your vision? Let me tell you; we spent hours and hours working on the 'Star Wars Font' idea."

"Onno, man, "our plant" found a place. I love the booklet that's it! And Tal, cool photos all are powering our plan! Ecstasy is departing out of our music! Cool Onno. Each fan will get a message, just beautiful."
Mono went on.
"Reality is hard; to live in reality even harder, but to flee reality is ecstasy."
Onno smiled about his comment.
"Yeah, I hope so too, that they will be flying." Tal sounded not quite as enthused as Mono acted.
"We want to inspire people; we need any help we can get Tal. By the way, Onno, did you already speak with Sentinel about all of the details?"
"No problem, that's the easy part."
"Yeah, I know that. But this will be our first album with Sentinel."
"Don't worry about it. Trust me."
Finally, he turned and said to Tal, "Okay, man, before you explode, show me your pictures."
Tal already had the pictures waiting in his hands.
He flipped through the top of the stack. "Tal, I already saw these photos."
"Continue please!"
"Oh, sorry," and he flipped through the rest of the stack.
"Wow, Tal Tabitha appears beautiful, these photos are good for any fashion magazine."
Mono acted completely happy and thus so looked everyone in the room. But he did not like to make a major business decision without a day or two to think about it.

"Okay, guys, I will let you know by Monday evening. Sorry, but this lasted a hard week for me. Is that cool for you?"
"Oh yeah, it's cool for me," Tal smiled.
"Onno do you have thoughts about it?"
"It's fine with me."
Work talk did finish so, as always, the conversation turned to partying.
Dance 2 Trance - "Hello San Francisco" happened to be beating from the stereo system in the room.
He asked both of them, "You guys have any plans for the weekend?"
Tal answered, "We should go to "Chemistry" on Saturday night. Marcello is playing. And on Sunday morning we should hit "After Energy Hours.""
Onno agreed.
"OK, I will see you guys Saturday night at "Chemistry." But before you leave, let us have a drink. We have something to celebrate."

Mono and Tabitha hired a taxi to the Escape club like they did almost every Saturday night. The Escape venue, on a corner of the Amsterdam's famous Rembrandt Square, the place hosted restaurants, pubs, and nightclubs.
"Mies, look how crowded it is outside!"
"Oh my god, babe, can you see Thijs somewhere at the door?"

"No, I can't see him! Maybe he isn't there, but he should be. Let's walk a little closer. Maybe he changed his hair from blue to green this week, and that's why we can't recognize him." Both loved it. While they walked towards the club, he took a long look around Rembrandt square. His gaze rested on Smokey's coffee shop on the opposite side of the plaza.
"Babe, let's go to Smokey's for a minute and buy some pot. I feel like smoking tonight."
As always, Smokey's crowded as the rest of the square. The doorman recognized the long-haired German, so they didn't wait more than thirty seconds. The owner greeted with the same friendliness at the weed counter, where he quickly bought his favorite pot. After the purchase, however, Smokey's seemed no longer entertaining for both of them. Less than fifteen minutes later, he and Tabitha appeared back at the front door of Escape. As they arrived at the door, Thijs the Dutch party promoter showed up calling Tabitha by her name.

"Quick, come here!" Thijs shouted.
The couple' waded through the sea of people and finally made it to the doorstep where Thijs greeted them with a friendly smile.
"How are you guys doing?"
"Excellent, thanks,"

Thijs acted as always very nice, especially to Tabitha.
He told her how gorgeous she looked and gave the
free tickets to Tabitha, not to Mono.
Mono noticed but let it slide, "Thanks a lot, Thijs."
Thijs grinned widely and said, "It's always a pleasure
to have you guys around."

Amsterdam natives often reminded Mono that the
Escape venue had been a Cabaret in Amsterdam's
earlier days.
The two-story building appeared still gorgeous and
ornate and always crowded with beautiful people.
Without question, Escape emerged as the hottest club
in Amsterdam on a Saturday night.
"Look, Tabitha, there are Angela, Sanni, and Wayne!"
"Yeah, Mies, and Nakka D, too," "Come on, let's go
over and say hi."
"Hi, guys!" Mono yelled. "What a party!"
They all smiled in agreement, but he could not hear a
word anyone had said. A normal conversation
seemed impossible, so he didn't bother to wait for any
answer.
"Come on, guys, let's go up to the second floor to the
Vitamin bar to drink juice."
Again, everyone agreed, and they all followed him up
the stairs.
"Look, guys, there is our buddy Tal!" Sanni shouted.
"Oh man, look how wasted he is!"
Tal sauntered over and nearly spilled his drink.

"You guys having fun?"
"Of course we are having a good time as always. How many drinks have you had, Tal?"
"Oh, I don't know, maybe three. Thijs handed me a few free drink tickets at the door over."
Hey, where's Onno?" Mono asked.
"He isn't here. When I called him, he appeared too tired, so he stayed at home."
"That's his fault," Nakka D said. "Onno never comes out; he always acted unwillingly to use energy on a Saturday night when I asked him to get out with all friends together." Nakka continued and asked Tal, "Who is this cute girl? I thought you were gay, man."
Everyone laughed, and the blood rushed to Tal's face. Mono interrupted the laughter, "Hey guys, that's not funny at all." Mono to Tal, "Hey, man, this wild guy over here is Nakka D. Do you know him? Don't take him seriously; he seems wasted."
Tal didn't answer but the girl with him, whose name occurred to be Sabine, said, "Oh, I know this Nakka D guy. We went to the same school in the South East together."
She seized Tal, knocked over the rest of his drink, and they both ran down towards the dance floor.

Tabitha appeared shaking her hot ass on the dance floor, grabbing the attention of everyone around her. She loved it, but for Mono, any place even close to the dance floor seemed way too loud these days. Mono tried to catch her attention and succeeded after about a minute. Mono signaled to her that he acted moving to the front of the club.

He left to find a quiet corner and ran right into Max.

"Brother! Oh, man, what's up?"

Max, with his sturdy body and bright smile, took him and gave him a big bear hug.

"Hey! What's up?"

"The same question I have, man. What's up with you? Jo told me that you played in London."

"Not for this weekend mate. I performed spinning at the Grasshopper last night, and tomorrow night I'm playing in Zaandam."

Mono took a sniff of the air around him and looked down.

"Uh oh, what do you have there in your hand, Max?"

Without waiting for an answer, Mono took Max's right hand and gripped hold of a big joint.

"Let me take a few puffs, man."

He took three quick hits.

In the meantime, Max asked him, "What's up with the records? Jo told me that everything seems ready to rock."

"Yeah, but please Max, not here. We'll have time to talk about it later. Man, this stuff makes my head spin."

"Haha, I know it. So, where is the rest of the crew?" Max asked.

At that exact moment, Tabitha jumped on Max's back and secured him with affection.
"Max! Max! How are you? Where's Gino? And where is your girlfriend?"
Nakka D jumped in front of Max, and he surrounded him on all sides. Max acted stoned and a little bit overwhelmed.
"Guys, you know what? I must admit that I love the attention, but you have to be careful with me. I look tough, but I break easily."
Everyone laughed, and the three guys began the usual party talk while Nakka D took his turn with the joint.
Finally, Max puffed the last hit and crushed the roach on the sticky floor. Maw looked around and asked him, "Where did Tabitha go?"
Right then, Sanni showed up out of nowhere and answered Max's question.
"Look, man, she's grooving at the highest point on the dance floor, like always."
Max laughed and gave Sanni a big hug.
"Hey, Sanni! Happy to see you, man! What are you up to later tonight?"
"We all want to go to the after party...."
The next question occurred inevitable and, as usual, aimed at Mono.
"Are we on the guest list?"
"No, Max," he answered, "but I am sure the guys from Magic Studio will be there so that it will be no problem."
Tabitha made her exit from the dance floor and seemed back in the conversation just in time to hear his answer.

"Yeah, Mies, but before we go to the after party we will stop at home for a little while, right?"
Not one of their friends could hold back a smile.

III

Call TV

The Pantharei Television studio located on Amsterdam's historic Prinsengracht canal, one of the loveliest streets in the world. From his office window, Daniel could see hundreds of boats floating down the water street throughout the summer.

But on that particular day, Daniel had no interest in the beautiful scenery. His attention stayed captured entirely by his partner Aniza the Persian designer, who emerged screaming at him from across the desk.

"We don't have enough girls for our shows! I already said it to you before Christmas, but you completely ignored me. It's almost New Year's Eve, and in little time, we have our fashion show. The showcase on TV in even less time! You keep telling me not to worry. Tell me, what are we going to do now?"

"How many girls canceled?" Daniel patiently asked.

"Daniel, you already know it! The worst part seemed that our live act wouldn't be available because of an accident."

"Yes, I know."

"Daniel, tell me the truth, please. Did you have an affair with Elisa?"

"What makes you think that?"

"Ever since we got the phone call about her problem, your face has been whiter than the wallpaper."

"No, Aniza, trust me, it has nothing to do with that."
"Okay, tell me what we're going to do. You said Mono is producing a new hottie."
"Yeah, he does. But I didn't call him like I promised. And, Aniza, if he joins our team, it isn't going to be for free."
"At this point Daniel, I don't care. This event is my first fashion show in Amsterdam and the first time that my designs are going to be on TV. The one thing I know for sure existed we are desperate. Let's get in touch with him. Please, call his office right now."
"Ok just give me a second to get my act together." Daniel picked up the phone and dialed the RW Records office number.
"It's Daniel, how are you?"
"Oh, Hi Daniel, can you please hold on for a second?" Olga put her hand over the receiver and whispered to Mono, "it's Daniel on the phone. Are you available?" Mono shook his head and whispered back, "What does he want?"
"Hi, Daniel, I'm back. Sorry about that. What's going on?"
Daniel acted little nervous and began out with some small talk. He struggled on the phone in the middle of describing all the food he ate at Christmas dinner when Olga interrupted him.
"Daniel, did you call here to talk about Christmas dinner? What can I do for you?"
"I got a little bit distracted sorry. Is Mono around? I would like to talk to him."

Olga liked the game. The truth seemed that she admired Daniel, but he acted always ignoring her. So now it happened to be a kind of payback for her, and she served to enjoy every second.
Finally, she gave up the teasing and told Daniel to call on Mono's private telephone.
"He is taking a break until New Years. Do you need his number?"
"No, Olga, thanks, I have that number. By the way, I'm having a fashion show at Escape. I'll send a bunch of tickets over to you at the office."
"Thanks, Daniel, that's very nice. I guess I will see you there, Happy Holidays!"
With "Happy Holidays," Daniel ended the conversation.
Mono appeared sitting behind his desk; Listening to Calvin Stones - "The Pool" and watching the conversation play out between Olga and Daniel.
After she had hung up the phone, Mono said to Olga, "I can see how much you just enjoyed that."
"Oh yeah, I had fun. And I also have tickets for Daniels fashion show."
"Oh, really you do?"
Mono had a little smirk on his face and continued.
"That means Daniel needs something we might have."
"Come on, when you are smiling like that, I know something is cooking in your brain."
"First tell me what he wanted."
"He said he needed to talk to you."
"He said what about?"
"I don't know; he didn't tell me. I assume it has something to do with his show."
Mono´s smirk turned into a grin.

"I bet that's what it's about."
"Come on, I'm curious. You knew that Daniel is eventually going to call you, didn't you?"
"He told me he would call me a while ago. If my feeling seems right, Daniel needs a little star for his show."
"How could you possibly know about that?"
"I have this image in my brain since a while already," he grinned.

Twenty minutes later, Mono occurred to sitting in front of his television when the phone began to ring. He knew who called. He picked it up after two rings and immediately said, "Hi, Daniel."
"Man, how did you know?"
"Olga told me that you would be calling. What can I do for you?"
Daniel skipped the small talk this time.
"Do you remember when we spoke about my show the other week?"
"Of course but I thought you would come by my office to finish the conversation."
"Yea, but everything went a little crazy around here, and I didn't make it. Sorry I didn't call and let you know."
"I know how it goes Daniel. It's all about the money."
"Well, actually, you got me. But you know our budget is tight this time."

"Anyway, Daniel, you should have called. I always take you seriously; don't treat me like that next time."
"Sorry. But to tell you the truth, I am in trouble right now. The Escape show is in a week and the showcase on Veronica TV in five days already."
"You're doing it on Veronica? An excellent channel, examined from every point of view. You have good contacts, Daniel."
"Come on, stop teasing me. I need your help. Is that new singer available for those days? Are you interested in having she perform her new song at these shows?"
"Is that all?"
"Well, we want her to model Aniza's clothing line on TV as well."
"OK, listen to me Daniel; I am at home for one hour more. Can you stop by my house? I need to know a little bit more about it."
"Sure, I will be at your house in 20 minutes."
Mono hung up the phone and switched over into thinking mood.

Tabitha spent most of her time in his house alone, in the fourth-floor atelier. For some odd reason, she relished the seclusion. Mono never appeared much bothered about it. He respected her wish of certain privacy in his house. After she had moved in he asked her one time why she loves to spend so much time in solitude, Tabitha gave a vague answer. She said it had something to do with the time she lived together with her mother in Utrecht, but she never explained any further.

Tabitha could hear Mono screaming from the living room. She has been plagued with longing and already making her way down the stairs anyway.

"Babe, please come down for a second!"

Tabitha stopped at the bottom of the staircase.

"Oh, you're already here. Sorry for screaming love. Listen, babe, Daniel just called, and I have some good news. We surprisingly can take your new song on TV!"

"Are you teasing me?"

"Daniel will be here in a few minutes, and I think we will close the deal. The central question appears to be, are you ready for it? Can you do it? Imagine - you will be performing in front of TV cameras as well as the studio audience. And at these moments won't be anyone available to help you. It is just you. It's live - television, and anything you do wrong will stay forever it's broadcasting. Think about it for a minute."

Tabitha needed approximately one second to make up her mind. Maybe one hundred thousand people, she imagined, all watching her perform?

"Of course I will do it!"

And with a smile on her face, she asked, "How much will Daniel pay?"
"Oh, Tabitha, I know your new actor face very well. First of all, I am sure you can do it. As for the money part, however, I guess it won't be too much. It's more of a promotional gig for you."
Before she could comment, the doorbell rang.
"That must be Daniel already. Babe, please open the door. And be a good girl."
Tabitha smiled and put on her Sunday face while she staggered down the narrow staircase. Rozalla - Everybody's Free started hitting from the stereo system in the room.

"Hartmut, wait for a second for me!"
"Harold, come on, I'm late. It's the last day of the year, and I don't want to hear anything anymore. I just want to get out of the damn studio."
"Yes, Hartmut, I understand, but I think you want to hear this. I have Raul on the phone."
"And what is so interesting about that? Come on; I want to leave."
Harold knew how to catch Hartmut's attention.
"Tabitha will be performing her song on Veronica at the "Call TV" show on January 3rd."
"No way, man, you're kidding!"
As Harold expected, Hartmut turned around and walked right back into the studio, grabbing the telephone out of Harold's hand.

"Raul," he said brusquely, "Hartmut here. Are you drunk already?"

"No, Hartmut, it's the truth. They are going to be on Veronica."

"Fuck man, this dude did it. Well... I guess this is good news for Magic Studio as well. I am euphoric; we have credits of the song."

Raul kept still talking, but Hartmut seemed not listening anymore. He ended the conversation and looked at Harold.

"And?"

Harold, calm like always, shrugged his shoulders. "Look, it's one more reason to celebrate tonight. I just don't want to be the one to give the news to Peter."

Suddenly Hartmut remembered one more thing he still had to do at the studio. He tossed his briefcase back on the table and took off his jacket.

"What's going on?" Harold asked, confused. "I thought you couldn't wait to get out of here."

"Yeah," Hartmut shrugged, "but I forgot about some people I need to call about tonight. And I can't wait until I get home to call, you know?"

Hartmut's excuse appeared weak to him, but Harold didn't push for a better explanation. He decided to get out of the studio and get started with the evening's festivities. So he slung his bag over his shoulder and walked towards the front door.

"Alright, Hartmut, I guess I will see you later tonight. Try not to stick around here too long. And don't forget the lights!"

"Yeah, yeah see you later!"

Hartmut waited until he was sure Harold had gotten away. He ran straight to the phone and dialed Peter's number. When he heard Peter's voice, he only had one thing to say.
"Peter, the show will be January 3, on Veronica's show "Call TV." Okay?"
"Thanks, man, I knew I could count on you."
Hartmut hung up the phone without saying goodbye and rushed out of the studio.

Eric lived two floors down from Magic Studios. He arrived as the smallest shareholder in the studio hierarchy, but he occurred to be one of their most valuable assets. He knew that nobody else at Magic Studio had his talent.
Eric appeared sitting in his small apartment, deep in thought and reliving some events from the first weeks at the studio. He tried to decide if he could call it a good year when the telephone rang and broke into his reverie.
Picking up the phone, Eric heard a very nervous Raul.
"Eric," he said breathlessly, "Mono called a few minutes ago. Tabitha is going to perform your song "Where Is My Love?" on TV!"
Eric floored.
"Which station?" he asked immediately.
 "Veronica!" Raul answered.

"Oh man, that's fucking great! But why didn't he call me? Is he still pissed that I edited the song without telling him first?"

"No, man, he's not mad at you at all. He said that he tried to call you, but your cell phone seemed offline."

"That's not possible! Oh, wait for a second, where is that damn thing? Here we go...fuck, it is turned off! I didn't do that! Maybe that chick Mandy did it. I can't believe it I am waiting for my mother to call as well."

"Mandy? Eric, you're mixing with Mandy? What happened to your girlfriend Wendy?"

"Raul, we're both having our fun with her. But that's none of your business. So anyway, what are your plans for this new year's evening?"

"I don't have much of a plan. I'm just hanging out with some friends."

"Well, in case I don't see you tonight, Raul, I wish you a happy new year. Oh yeah, one last thing, what's the date for the show?"

"January 3."

It appeared to be already 5 PM on December 31, but Peter dialed Pete's office number anyway. He decided it seemed to be worth a shot, and it happened to be a business call after all. Peter reached a voice mailbox, so Peter hung up and dialed Pete's cell phone number. This time he acted successfully. Pete picked up the phone, and it occurred evident from the background noises that he apparently has no time.

"Hey, Pete, it's Peter here, how are you doing?"
"I am a good man just great as always Happy New Year! I'm in the middle of something right now, but what can I do for you?"
Pete the Dutch VIP knew Peter from his "Energy Hours" parties. "Thanks, Pete I only need a few minutes of your time. I am sure you are pretty busy."
"No, Peter," he interrupted, "I always have time for you, you know that!"
Peter laughed to himself. This time the special treatment emerged successfully.
"Thanks again, man. Listen, I have a question. You work with the Veronica Channel, right?"
"Yeah…"
Pete hesitated to answer. In fact, he worked with the Veronica radio, not the television channel. He preferred to keep quiet about the detail.
"Okay," Peter said quickly. "Well, do you know anything about a singer, her artist name is Tabitha, and she is supposed to be performing on Veronica's "Call TV" morning show on January 3rd?"
Pete had no idea what he intends talking about to him. "I would need to check our detailed programming for that day." He answered.
"I am sure you have lots of different performances planned for that day. Anyway, listen, I know this girl. She recorded in Magic Studio recently and man, Pete, I heard her sing, and I just had to warn you about her quality. I want to give you a chance to save the show. The best for you guys is to cancel her appearance."

Pete acted surprised at what he heard, especially because of the timing. Why Peter showed calling on New Year's Eve with this kind of wish? Pete did searching for words to comforts his friend but went for the easiest way.

"That bad, huh? Thanks for letting me know, Peter. I will see what I can do. There isn't much time, you know."

"Yes, I know, but trust me, it is worth your while."

"You got it. I'm sorry Peter, but I really should get going. See you at Escape on Sunday."

"Like always, man."

Peter hung up, satisfied with the conversation.

"Toffyyyyy!"

"Mono! Hi, man!"

"How ended up your New Year's, man?"

"Oh, don't ask. We had a show in Hilversum and, well, you know those black guys..." he trailed off.

"I know some of them very well," he commiserates. He could tell that Toffy the Dutch dancer acted itching to tell a story, so he decided to appease him. Anyway, Toffy always had a good story to tell.

"Alright, man, tell me what happened."

"Well," Toffy began, "after the show, some blond bitches appeared waiting for us so of course Vincent and I had to check it out. All three lived in Utrecht, so we had a hell of a lot of fun. But I lost every ounce of my energy, and I didn't get to see any of the fireworks. And on top of that, I slept for twenty-four hours. I'm telling you, man; I just woke up."

"I feel sorry for you today," Mono teased. "But seriously, I'm sorry for waking you up."

"No, no, it's cool. Tell me what I can do for you."

"Well, tomorrow Tabitha is performing her new song on TV."

"Yeah, I heard about that. As you know, Toffy here gets all of the entertainment news in this city."

"I know, man," "but that is not the point."

"So what is the point? Do you need me to hold her hand?"

"You are a funny guy, Toffy. Maybe you should do that. But let's be serious for a second. Friday night she will perform at Aniza's fashion show."

"Oh yeah," Toffy said, "I know that as well."

"But what you don't know is that Daniel occurred to be in a complicated situation when he hired Tabitha for the show, I asked for the image rights for the show in return."

"What are you going to do with that? There's little that exciting about a fashion show from a newcomer like Aniza."

"Oh, trust me; there is something very exciting about it for me. We are going to record Tabitha's performance for a sequence of a video clip. Now we are getting to your part, Toffy. I need some professional talent, and of course, I am thinking about you."

"I appreciate the thought. I will be busy on Friday night, but let me make some phone calls, and I will arrange some great dancers for you."

"That's cool, Toffy, thanks. There is one more thing. The budget is small, and I cannot spend more than I do for an average show, even if is it for a video clip sequence."

"No problem, brother, but either way, I get ten percent commission of the gross payment."

"I can agree on that."

"Tomorrow you will have your dancers; I can promise you that. I will call you later and give you all the details." Snap - "Rhythm is a dancer" appeared hitting from the stereo at the RW Records office.

"Faith, long times no talk!"

"Wow, Frank, it has been a long time."

"I know it. So, tell me, how is the weather out there in Los Angeles?"

"It's hazy today. But for sure it's not nearly as cold as New York."

"It's not so cold today in New York, but of course the sky is gray as always in the winter."

"Okay, so what can I do for you? I am guessing you didn't call me today just to find out if the sun appeared shining in LA."
Faith, the American smart girl, acted in a hurry to leave her apartment but she didn't want to push him. Frank happened to be a good friend from her Yale college times, and it always seemed nice to hear his voice.
"Nope, you are right. The thing is I ran into DJ Peran the other day. He appeared visiting his brother in New York, and he told me that you guys are compiling a progressive trance playlist together for the U.S. market. It sounded interesting; I thought you could enlighten me a little bit."
"Frank, come on, a small trance project idea from a little company in L.A. is nothing for the big news, probably not even for the Village Voice."
"I wouldn't say that," Frank continued. "Not when the name of the label sounds so interesting. What are you guys up to these days?
"Man, you are grasping at straws here. But I guess that's your job. Tell me one thing - From where do you know DJ Peran in the first place and why begun you talking to him about his projects?"
"Faith, this is a secret and part of my job. But moving on, what is your sister doing these days?"
She noted the way Frank skillfully changed the subject.

"Status quo Jennifer continues working on her acting out here in LA. She is doing very well with her latest play, and we are confident that she will hit it big any day now. In the meantime, she is also doing some supporting acts to pad her resume. But you know as well as anyone; the business is tough as hell. Anyway, Frank, I would love to catch up some more my partner is coming in from Amsterdam today, and I am already late for the airport."

"No problem. I will stay tuned and follow up on the album."

"Do what you want. Although a little marketing help is always appreciated."

After Frank had said goodbye, Faith hung up the phone and rushed to the bathroom. She acted nervous about being late, but she couldn't shake the weird feeling she had after the phone call. Frank didn't answer her questions, and it didn't make any sense. Maybe Mono would know more.

Driving on the crowded 405 towards LAX, she was singing along to her favorite Guns N Roses album and playing the drums against the steering wheel. Some things would never change. She finally exited the highway and passed the McDonald's on the corner of Sepulveda. For a second she thought to herself, "Should I grab a hamburger?" But after checking her watch, she decided against it.

Mono's plane seemed to be late; Faith began regretting her decision not to stop for a snack. Right then she saw him coming out of customs with a big smile on his face. Mono saw her immediately and ran over to her with outstretched arms.

They exchanged a big hug and friendly greetings.

"It's so sweet to see you again Faith!"
"How ended up to be your flight?"
"It ended up shitty as always."
She smiled at his predictable response and grabbed one of his smaller bags out of his hand before he could protest. Both began walking towards the parking garage.
"I hate to fly, and there is nothing I can do about it. Maybe in the future, we will be able to beam from one point in the universe to another. But until then, I will always have that crappy feeling in my stomach whenever I board a flight." Mono stopped in his tracks and took a long look at Faith. She blushed lightly.
"Wow, you look great, Faith! What's your secret?"
"It's easy. No smoking, healthy food, and some workouts here and there. You still smoke those cancer sticks, don't you?"
"No," "I quit. I swear. And do you want to know the truth? It was only for you."
"Come on; you're kidding."
"No, I'm serious. I began to be affected if you are telling me always how horrible cigarettes are for me."
"I don't believe you. You will never stop smoking. But anyway," Faith changed the subject, "How is everything in Amsterdam? Tell me what kind of trouble you've been getting into lately."
They exchanged sly smiles.
"Well, actually, it's a lot of work out there for sure. But I will tell you everything later. Where the hell is the car?"
"Relax, huh? It's not so far."

The car stuck in Friday afternoon traffic on Los Angeles's infamous highway 405.

"Stop and go, stop and go, this shit never changes. Man, how long have we been sitting in the car already?"

"Forty-five minutes." I guess it's not too slow today as other days, but I swear, this highway is getting more crowded every month of the year. So tell me, should we go to your apartment first, or straight to the office?"

"Drive to the apartment; I need a quick shower."

"Do we have any plans for the day?"

"We have our meeting for this afternoon. How long you're going to stay in L.A. this time?"

"Well, I'm not so sure how long I will stay. It depends a lot on our progress. Do you have any news?"

"It's funny; actually, a friend from New York called me this morning. Frank is a freelance writer and is trying to get his articles placed in the big papers. He asked me about Peran's album project."

"These are surprising news indeed."

"He met DJ Peran in New York City. Our Label name caught his attention."

"It's fascinating."

"Yeah, that's what I thought. I did kind of hoped DJ Peran had mentioned anything about the freelance writer to you?"

Mono thought for a while. "I know the guy; I met him together with Peran, at Eric's recording studio in the Hollywood Hills past year. What a Small world. So what did you say to your friend today?"

"I told him there is no story; we occurred to be not even exciting enough for the Village Voice."

Mono laughed, "Good name, it exists so far as I remember. Anyway, let's keep in touch with him."
Faith kept talking, but Mono didn't hear a thing.
Mono seemed falling asleep. Thirty minutes later, the car pulled up to North Argyle and Franklin, in the Hollywood Hills.
She nudged him softly and whispered, "Hey, wake up Mono, we're home."
His blue eyes appeared glazed when they popped open, and he had to look around to orient himself.
"Oh, "I didn't even realize that I slept the final minutes of the ride. I guess it was a long flight for me. In two hours, I will meet you at the office, okay?"
"Perfect. And, it's very cool to have you here again."
"Faith, it's very cool to be back."

Mono walked up the stairs of his apartment complex, "How nice it is to be back in California. The air smells different" talking to an imagined third person.
"Mono, Mono! I have your mail!"
Mono turned around and saw his favorite caretaker yelling up to him to the second floor.
"How long are you going to stay?" she yelled again.
"You know what?" Mono yelled back, "I haven't even been here for two hours yet. But perhaps I will stay for a couple of weeks."
"I checked your apartment every week, just like I promised."

"That's very kind, thank you. Let me get settled here I will pick up my mail later." Mono went on.

"And if I ever get a Grammy Award," Inez, I promise I will mention you in my acceptance speech."

"I will be waiting," Inez smiled.

Mono headed straight towards his place satisfied to find all things he needs for now. As a robot, he switched on the sound system in the living room. Dance 2 Trance - "Power of The American Natives" playing helped Mono to get in a perfect mood. Mono inspected apartment, room by room, and found everything exactly as he had left it. Mono picked up the phone and dialed a cell phone number. "Hi, Steve, it's me, Mono."

"Where are you, man?"

"I'm back in town. Please, Steve, don't ask me how long I will stay. I honestly don't know, and every single person I've seen today has already asked the same question."

"Don't worry my friend, "I invite you to join us for a barbecue tomorrow afternoon at my house."

"Where is the new house?"

"Oh, you are too funny. The house in Laguna Hills, it's still the same."

"Sorry Steve it's been awhile I thought that maybe you finally made the big move from Orange County to LA."

"No I didn't and I never will L.A. is a great city, but I love living in Laguna Hills."

"Well, Steve you must have been reading my mind. A barbecue sounds great. If it's okay with you, I will bring my partner Faith."

"Of course it's okay. How is Faith doing these days?"

"She is doing great she is the heartbeat of my business."
"Amsterdam is it still there?"
"Yes Steve it's still there, and it's waiting for your next visit."
"Don't worries I will be in Amsterdam with some friends of mine either before or after the Cannes Film Festival I don't know yet."
"So we have a date."
"Yes, we've got a date."
"Well, I am writing it in my agenda right now. 'Steve Salomon, the American investor, is coming to Amsterdam soon.'"
"Man you can count on it."
"Yes I know," Mono laughed, "and so can all of the girls in Amsterdam."
Steve acted laughing too. Steve brought the conversation to a close.
"Sorry bro but I have to leave the house right now."
"Okay, it's no problem. I will see you on Saturday for some American style barbecue. Take care, man."
Mono tore off his smelly airplane clothes and jumped into a steaming shower.

Less than an hour later, Mono drove in his old Jaguar along Hollywood Boulevard. Took over fifty-five minutes stop and go to get him to Beverly Hills.
Faith looked up when Mono entered the office.
"You look totally stressed out."

"I will never get used to this traffic in Los Angeles."
"Come on; please relax. I already made you a coffee,"
Snap - "Do you see the Light" - Dance 2 Trance Mix
played hitting in the room.
Faith had already set up the conference table; her
folders appeared in the usually organized piles.
"First things first," tell me everything that is
happening in Amsterdam. I am very curious to hear
the stories from your mouth."
It took Mono a little moment to get comfortable and
to get in the right mood. He seemed smiling and
acted searching a document between his papers.
"What is it," Faith asked.
"Anyway, I just got the info right before my scheduled
flight. The "Zenith Pacha" album is confirmed. Pacha
sent their logo to RW Records. We are even allowed
playing around with it. By the way, before I forget,
everyone sends you greetings."
"Oh, that's nice."
"Well, you are a beautiful person."
"They sent it?" "That is great."
"Yes, it is huge, but a lot of planning in the coming
months."
"It seems an excellent decision to sign "Zenith" to this
mixed compilation album deal."
"It's a lot of work in the summer. We concentrate and
stay focus on the "Hot Weekend Amsterdam" project
for now."
"It's the most critical, right?"
The plan, "our force" plants "our plant" into the art of
the records. It's crucial for our whole project."

"I saw the prints the garden is excellent, could work. Holland continues the land of the Tulips after all." Faith answered and smiled.

Mono enjoyed few sips of his coffee and continued. "Tabitha performed on TV. She modeled at a fashion show in Amsterdam. She did well."

"I know that you told me about a new artist you want to promote."

"I want to sign Eric Nouhan to an exclusive album deal. The album is the new project."

"That's great! Something we can promote in America?" Mono made his thinking face. "We do not have the resources for it yet. Don't you agree?"

Faith appeared smiling, "Without proper resources, nothing goes. I agree."

"I am slightly more optimistic with Peran's planned mixed compilation album."

"What do you mean?"

"It could emerge as our chance to sell a trance music compilation album in record stores across America."

"When we know the stars of the playlist?"

"Patience we need, "our plant" needs to be in the right place first; we need to tinker a lot. It's all about the right timing. With Peran we signed the master of the sounds already. Let's eat the colossus one piece at the time*."

Faith stopped taking notes in her black leather agenda.

"Okay, now, that's everything?

"Not really," Mono continued with a smile. "We are producing a new song for Tabitha, planned to be a single song CD. Different mixes of the song we launch at both confirmed compilations."

Faith stopped writing to think about what Mono just said.
"Are you sure about it, isn't it a bit late for this addition?"
"As you already know since a while, we tried to license B.B.E. - "Seven Days and One Week" exclusive for the Benelux, as the medium for our trance-mission without success. Tabitha will be the star of the records. We will plaque 15000 exiting "Hot Weekend Amsterdam" posters around the Netherlands at prime locations, with Tabitha's beautiful being on them as the eye catcher. Plus place ads in some trendy magazines. The action shall initiate the growing up of "our plant." Furthermore, secure a fast multiplication of her spirit in the future."
Faith nodded, smiled and continued scribbling quickly. Mono could talk about so many different things without pausing between topics. Mono had the ability to keep all the projects in perfect order in his head.
"Faith, in case you get confused, I will email the production sheets to you.
"Haha, I appreciate it."
"Are you ever going to find some time to sleep?"
"Not much at the moment. We have a lot to wrap up before we have a chance to accomplish our goal in the Netherlands."
"Yeah, I know, what is going to happen with Tabitha?"
"She doesn't want to work in America. I don't have an answer yet."

IV

Kiss the Future

What's new in Los Angeles? I'm curious too!"
"Well, after that disaster with Robert, I had to start all over from scratch with our website, and it looks like our new group of freelancers is getting the hang of things."
Faith took a deep breath and continued her discourse. Mono concentrated on every word Faith said, of course, he did not write down a thing.
"Concerning DJ Peran's planned compilation record; I want to start working on a good distribution deal for America. Conduct some research about it."
Mono stood up from his chair and looked out the window. He kept watching the cars cruising down Santa Monica Boulevard, but he never lost his concentration.
"It's never too early; I agree you should start working on it. But with caution, we don't want to kill the project before we begin it." "I understand what you are talking about it. I just want to test the waters. "
"It sounds good for the start. But I bet you will be the happiest when you are back in Miami, right?"
"For sure it's been awhile since I've been around all of my friends and I'm starting to miss my mom."
"Your sister is still living in LA, right?"

"Yes, and we will see her tonight for dinner if you don't mind."
"I would love to see her again. How is Jennifer doing these days?"
"She is doing great. I won't go into details about her acting career because it will spoil our dinner conversation."
"Faith amusing you should be nicer. She is your sister, you know. So tell me, when exactly will you leave for Miami?"
"There is nothing left for me to do here anymore. When you leave, I will leave too. But don't worry; I won't leave before I have everything organized in Los Angeles."
"I'm not worried. I have faith in you.
She smiled when he managed to work her name into the conversation.
Mono always enjoyed watching her.
"But now that we caught up, I think you know what I want to do next."
"Yeah, yeah, you mean Starbuck's, don't you? Jeez, are you still addicted to that stuff?"
"I'm not addicted! It's just that Starbuck's is the best!"
She shook her head at yet another one of his addictions. She teased him, but she did enjoy sitting and watching people at their favorite Starbuck's on Sunset.

"Let's sit outside." The partners' parked the car on the side of the building and walked together toward the tree-ringed Starbuck's patio.

The afternoon had arrived one of the few times of the day when view empty tables were available.

"OK, no problem, we can sit right here."

Mono put his briefcase on top of the table closest to the sidewalk, "I will go in and get the coffee for us. What do you want?"

"I'm not in the mood for coffee right now. Can you get me a tea instead? I like that spicy black tea they have here."

Mono nodded and began walking towards the building when he heard a noise.

"Is that my phone continues making that weird sound?"

Faith shrugged, and they both chuckled when they saw few different hands simultaneously grabbing for phones. It seemed Faith attended the call.

Mono appeared back five minutes later with a coffee in one hand and tea in the other. He saw as Faith placing his phone back down on the table.

"Guess what? Your friend Thomas just called from Sao Paulo."

"Sao Paulo? It is late over there."

"Not really, Thomas said he wants to talk to you tomorrow 11 AM, Sao Paulo time."

"You see? Everyone is stealing my sleep! I will confirm later by email with him."

They sipped the hot drinks and fell into their L.A. Starbuck's ritual. Mono began the conversation this time.

"Check out the people at the table next to us. Who do you think they are?"
Faith acted laughing, "Yep, for sure they are actors, very famous people."
"And look, the table on your right, they are writing a screenplay."
Both agreed that Starbuck's on Sunset appeared to be the best place in town for people watching. "This is nice just to sit here on a Friday afternoon, get some sun on my face, have a nice conversation with you, and drink my favorite coffee for a change. What is on your mind while you sit here?"
"Well, I think that L.A. people are crazy, but for sure this is entertaining. And yes, I missed sitting here with you and talking, even if it means I have to support the Starbuck's Corporation."

Mono sipped on his second coffee tall when Faith picked up the conversation.
"Sorry for coming back to the subject of work, but is there a problem with your friend?"
"Everything with Thomas is fine. But let see what he has to say tomorrow. Let's just enjoy the sun and all this great entertainment on Sunset Boulevard. Oh, I almost forgot, what are your plans for tomorrow afternoon?"
"Why?"
"We are invited to Steve Salomon's house for a barbecue."

"That sounds great; we should go. I want to ask you for a long time already what's up with that guy Salomon anyway. Where did you meet him?"

"That's a funny story. One year ago in Cannes, at the Film Festival, I stayed in his apartment for a couple of days. A friend had invited me, and at the end of the story, I found out that it happened to be Steve who provided the place for me. On the first day, he assembled his guests in front of a local ATM. To make festival cash presents to each of us. I acted very weirdly this moment I couldn't close my mouth because of the surprise. We became friends after. Last summer I appeared as a guest at his house a few times. He became our first angel investor. The present you know."

"Where does Steve Salomon live?"

"Steve owns a house in a super cute typical American neighborhood in Laguna Hills, Orange County. Hey, you already finished your tea!

Do you want another one?"

"No, thanks, I have to pee. You know me."

"Well, I don't think I can handle a third, so maybe I should head home to relax a little bit. When are we meeting up with your sister?"

"I figured we would meet Jennifer at around eight tonight."

"Is it possible to change it to nine?"

"Let me call her first, but I think so."

"And where are we going to meet?"

"I thought we would pick you up at your apartment and after we will all go to Thai-American on Sunset."

"This is an excellent idea. This place has the best Pad Thai in town."

The Sound Quest studio on the far outskirts of Amsterdam existed as one of the hottest spots in the Netherlands for recording dance music. Gino the American DJ, the other half of the Funky Fakirs and Max seemed thrilled to hear that Jo had made them an appointment to record at the legendary place.
Max stood in front of the mixing board, squinting at the sound levels when he saw the color drain from Gino's face.
"Max," Gino screamed across the studio, "I cannot believe it! These DAT tapes here only have thirty minutes recording time!"
It occurred Max's turn to lose the color in his face.
"Oh my god, "are you sure?"
Max ran from the mixing board over to where Gino stood in front of the DAT recorder.
"Max, I am positive. Look right here. Thirty minutes!"
At first, Max could only shake his head back and forth in disbelief.
"Gino, what the hell are we going to do? It means we are going to have to start all over again with our recording session another day!"
"Wait," "hold on a second. You know what we can do? We can record the first CD on two DAT tapes and then when finished; we can edit everything on the computer."
Max continued to shake his head and stare at the ground.
"Man! Why didn't we check this out before we began?"
"Are you asking me, Max?"
Gino acted pointing his finger in Max's face.

"Don't blame me for this crap. I specifically bought
sixty minute DAT tapes for our recording."
Both 'The Funky Fakirs' acted silently in thought.
Both heads continued swimming with desperate
solutions.

"Fuck," Gino finally decided, "I am calling Jo."
"Gino, wait! I have another idea. Why don't you just
call Olga and tell her that we need another day at the
studio."
"I already thought about that, but it isn't possible.
The guy from the studio already told me that we have
to be finished here by tomorrow morning at eight at
the latest. They already booked the studio for the next
seven days."
Again Max had no answer. He could only assess the
situation for what it seemed.
"Fuck," Max said. "That means we have fourteen
hours left to finish here and we don't have any DAT
tapes."
Max seemed to react clasping clumps of his hair in
frustration. All of a sudden he smiled.
He remembered that one of his friends the British
Andy had DATs at his house in the city.
"Look, Gino," "I'll take the car right now and drive to
Andy's house to pick up the tapes. I will turn back as
quickly as possible."
Gino appeared not quite as confident with Max's
latest solution.

"Max, I am anxious that we are going to fuck everything up here. You know Mono, man. Mono happened to be very fucking picky, and he will kick our asses if the recording is not final work by tomorrow. We both know that Mono is giving us a big opportunity here. We should try and come up with a better solution than your Andy dude."

"Gino, it's not like Amsterdam has a Domino's DAT delivery! You can get weed delivered in 20 minutes here, but that's about it!"

"Okay, Max, all right, just calm down. But please call this guy before you leave, at least find out if Andy stayed at home."

"I already spoke to him for a while this morning. Andy mentioned that today looked to be his girlfriend's birthday and he is making her a small party at their house. For sure he is still at home."

"Max, I'm not as sure as you are, but what else can we do? Let's give it a shot."

Faith seemed deep in sleep when a strange noise penetrated her dreams. Finally, the realization hit her that the telephone appeared ringing. For a second she thought, "Fuck it," and didn't move. After two more rings, she groaned and reached across the bed to pick up the phone. She heard his voice coming through the receiver.

She squinted at her alarm clock and saw it was only nine in the morning. Mono appeared talking, but she couldn't understand a word nor could she coherently respond. All she could muster was a weak mumble.
"It's nine in the morning! What do you want?"
"I know I am so sorry about it. I guessed you would be sleeping, but I needed to talk to you for a minute. Listen, everything has changed. I just got off the phone with Thomas in Sao Paulo."
She acted still groggy, and her voice sounded like a little foghorn.
"Oh yeah," she mumbled again, "I forgot you guys had that phone meeting. So tell me what is so important that you woke me up on a Saturday morning?"
"I'm sorry," he apologized again. "But Thomas seems surprisingly ready to negotiate a contract with us, and we need to discuss some things first."
She could see through the slits in her blinds that outside appeared the beginning of a beautiful Los Angeles day. She asked him if it could wait until later in the morning.
He apologized yet again and explained that it couldn't wait that long. "Okay," Faith conceded, "where are we going to meet?"
Mono suggested their old breakfast joint on Ventura. She agreed and promised to be there in an hour.

Faith acted irritated from the wake-up call, but she thoroughly enjoyed the early morning drive down Studio City's Ventura Boulevard. After parking her Honda in front of the diner, Faith walked straight to the back patio. She remained sure she would find Mono sitting at one of the picnic style tables in the shade under some trees. And she selected right. Normally Faith would have a friendly greeting and a hug for him, but on this Saturday morning, the first words out of her mouth were less than friendly.
"You are killing me, man. I need my sleep, and you know that!"
His big smile calmed her down immediately. Mono spoke very softly and slowly.
"Come on Faith, please, sit down and have a coffee. Eat something sweet, and I promise the day will be your friend."
She sat down under the leaves and saw that the table covered with delicious looking food.
"Oh, you already ordered. And you even got some toast with my favorite blueberry jelly! Mmm."
Mono laughed because she acted licking her lips when she saw the jelly.
"You said one hour, and I know how you are always on time."
Twenty minutes later, she happened to be stuffed and finally capable of holding a conversation. "You slept at all the night before."
"After I came home last night," "I had a couple of beers and sat by myself, enjoying the view of the city from my apartment. I fell asleep for a few hours."
All of a sudden, Mono jumped to an entirely different subject.

"That appeared to be a nice dinner last night, seemed not it?"
Mono had a habit of suddenly changing the topic of the conversation. Faith politely answered his question but pushed him back to the original subject.
"Yes, my sister and I enjoyed the evening. But I didn't get up at the crack of dawn to talk about our last night. Tell me what is going on with Thomas."
Mono signaled to the waitress to fill up his coffee mug. He looked back at Faith and answered her question.
"Here is the reason. Music Bank Brazil in Sao Paulo wants to negotiate investments in DJ Peran's forthcoming mixed album. MBB want to release it. The business conditions will be perfect. The album will cost our company around $3.00 per unit in North-America, ready for distribution and that including taxes.
The only condition we would have to place, pay in advance an order of 2000 units of Peran's forthcoming compilation record. We can't produce for this price in America. What do you think?"
Faith put on her thoughtful face. It took her a while to respond to his question.
"I think if we save money it is good but complicated to execute. Brazil is a third world country, full of surprises, does not forget it. When are we going to negotiate the contract?"
"We will take it into account of course. We will meet Thomas in Sao Paulo next month."
Mono said this rather matter-of-factly as if it did nothing.
But Faith did not fall for his subtlety.

"Hold on a second, did I hear you right? We, do I have to be there as well?
That will change our entire schedule! Did you even think about that?"
"This is why I called you so early this morning. And to answer your other question, of course, you have to be there with me. I think that together we can make this deal even bigger and better."
"Why didn't you tell me what you began assuming yesterday? We continued talking about business in the office for hours!"
"Because yesterday nothing had happened yet and nothing seemed possible."
"Fine, what exactly do you mean by 'bigger and better'?"
"We need content for our future distribution division. MBB has a catalog of 1000 songs of all genres. It's a decent number to start. Let's try to get a deal for America."
"You think that Thomas will give the distribution to us? That would be perfect for us."
"It would also be a great opportunity for Thomas. But we will see what happens when we have our meetings in Sao Paulo."

Until February there isn't a lot of time. How are we going to do all of this?"
Mono signaled to the waitress to fill up his coffee mug again.

Faith always acted especially nervous when thinking about money or deadlines and she couldn't hide the anxiety in her voice.

"Yes I know," Mono calmly replied. He had the opposite reaction to this kind of stress. "I will be leaving L.A. sooner than I had anticipated."

"What exactly are you thinking?"

"I guess I will have to fly out next Tuesday. So we have today, tomorrow, and Monday to make the plan together.

It should be enough time to set up our schedule for the next weeks."

"What about the barbecue?"

"I have to call Steve. He will understand it."

"When do you think you will leave for Miami?"

"I believe that if you leave on Tuesday, I will get a flight out on Wednesday. I need to check with American this afternoon. But, come on," she begged, "think about that barbecue for a minute. I wanted to meet your Steve. And we could use a little bit of fun."

"Okay, okay, you convinced me. I do hate to give up the good food anyway. Let's get the check here and go to Melrose for a quick shopping trip.

We can drive straight to Orange County."

"Wait, I know you already have everything planned, but let's do it a little differently. You go to Melrose alone and do your shopping. In two hours you can pick me up at Jennifer's place."

On the streets of Beverly Hills, it seemed to be a day like every other day. The sky appeared baby blue, and the sun continued shining. Tourists leisurely crossed the streets while business people rushed down the sidewalks in between meetings. Mono enjoyed the scene from ten stories above the street, in the office, he shared with Faith.

He reluctantly took his attention away from the window and walked back into the hectic work environment. Like every time Mono visited the office, the activity left him jittery. He felt out of control. Faith acted much more comfortable with the L.A. freelancers.

"Your plane is leaving in three hours," Faith urged him. "We need to get moving here."

Mono knew she seemed to talk to him, but he didn't hear what Faith said because he had just picked up the ringing telephone.

"Hold that thought for a second, please, Faith. I have Jo here on the phone."

"Jo, listen to me. Don't worry. I will be back in town tomorrow, and we will have enough time. Oh, and please say hi to Olga for me."

While he continued telling Jo not to worry, Faith could see the grave concern on his face. Something very wrong appeared.

"Your face just turned completely white! What happened?"

"Well, The Funky Fakirs couldn't record our music past Friday. I still don't know what went wrong in the studio, but I will get the rest of the story tomorrow in Amsterdam. We lost money and time. Trust me, though; everything will be fine, you know the plan."

"Everything will be great, like always," she repeated, "but not if we don't get our butts down to the car right this second. And I suggest you start praying for some luck on the 405."
For him, however, this last minute run to LAX seemed already a routine.
Mono had a better solution.
"Let's just take Sepulveda the whole way down to the airport.
I promise you we will get there in time."

"Is there any work left for to do?"
"Let me think about it for a second. As soon as you have a chance, prepare a budget spreadsheet with all the expenses for our Sao Paulo trip. I guess that's it. But honestly, I feel guilty giving you all of the work. I know that between L.A., Miami and Sao Paulo, you are barely going to have enough time to breathe."
"I can handle the work," Faith assured him. "We are both going to be working eighteen-hour days for the next few weeks."
Mono happened to be right about the drive.
Sepulveda looked clear of traffic, and they had arrived at the airport with a few minutes to spare.
Both appeared listening to music in front of Terminal 7 in the car and nodded their heads to the beats of Laconic - "Hooch."
Mono turned to look at Faith in the driver's seat with a distinct smile on his face.

"Thanks so much for the ride. Thank you for everything as always. You can just drop me off right here at the United Airlines departure gate. That way you can hopefully avoid rush hour driving back on Sepulveda now."
They exchanged a big hug. The first time, the thought of leaving this woman in L.A. gave him a strange feeling in the pit of his stomach.
While Mono tried to understand what his body acted telling him, he just barely heard, "I hope you have a safe flight and I will see you in Sao Paulo in few weeks."
"I hope you also have a safe flight to Miami tomorrow."

Olga kept relaxed sitting in front of her computer when she felt another presence in the room. Olga looked up and saw Mono with his clothes and hair still disheveled from the overnight plane flight. He dropped his bags in the doorway. The CD sound system streamed Dance 2 Trance - "Take a Free Fall" in the room.
"Wow," "that seemed a quick trip to L.A.!
Don't tell me you missed the crappy weather here that much!"
"No, Olga. I missed, you so much that I just had to get on the next plane back to Amsterdam."
Mono acted grinning at his joke.

"Seriously, though, there emerged no way I could leave you guys alone all of these weeks. From what I hear, we've got a few disasters on our hands.
But before we get into details, let me grab a coffee. I already have a headache."
Mono turned around as quickly as he had come in and headed to the kitchen downstairs. Olga ran down after him. She did not go to let him get away that easily. When both got to the basement, she immediately got down to business.
"Gino suggested we should change to a different recording studio. Do you know where he wants to record now? Oh, and while you are at it, can you make coffee for me too?"
"No problem at all. You are welcome."
Mono poured a second spoon of beans into the machine.
"And yes, I know where Gino wants to record, but right now I can't remember the name. I thought Gino sent you all the info in an email."
"Yeah, I need to go check again. Anyway, the DAT they recorded at Sound Quest is in your recorder.
"OK cool, let's play it then." Both went back upstairs to the office.

Mono could see the rain splashing against the window. He acted drumming on his knees to the beats of "Seven Days and One Week."

"Oh my god," he thought to himself, "Welcome back to Amsterdam."

On his desk waited at least a dozen unopened letters. He left the mail untouched and instead turned his attention to the computer.

Olga could not understand how he expressed no concern about the Gino and Max disaster.

"Are you just hiding your anxiety?"

"No, Olga, everything in life has a reason. Here is Gino's email."

Mono pointed at the computer screen.

"See? Gino already has booked a studio for tomorrow. So everything should be okay. Actually, can you please give him a call, so he knows that the appointment is confirmed? Tell him I will be there at two in the afternoon.

By the way, where worked Jo this noon?"

"Jo had an appointment at Free Record."

Olga looked down at Mono's desk. "Oh yeah, Jo also mentioned that he left a note for you on your desk."

"Yes, I already saw the note. I can't believe this whole FedEx mystery."

"Yeah, Jo did telling me the whole story."

"Whatever, it sounds like everything is okay, at least for now,"

"Yeah, I guess.

Oh, I almost forgot, Tabitha, will be in the next issue of Elle France, as one of the newcomer models of the year."

"Wow it did work out; does Tabitha already know about it?"

"Yes, when Tal told me, Tal mentioned that he would be calling her next."

"Of course, man. Knowing Tal, I bet he enjoyed telling her the good news."
"Tabitha stays upstairs right now in your apartment."
"Yes, I know. I will be up there in a minute too. It developed a hectic trip, and I need to relax a little. Listen, I will be back in the office around two."
Mono shifted his attention back to the computer screen and checked a few more emails, but after five minutes he couldn't concentrate anymore. Olga had not moved since the end of their conversation, and her eyes remained focused on the spot on the wall.
"Olga, I can tell by the look on your face that something is bothering you. What's going on?"
"Yeah, you're right, something bothering me.
Listen, Jo told me that you are planning on working in America frequently."
Mono acted not expecting to hear this from Olga. Mono had been putting off this conversation since Olga begun working for RW Records and he felt guilty.
"Oh, Jo told you? He is reading a lot of simple information I gave him into something huge." Mono said innocently.
"Yeah, and I can't help but wonder what is going to happen to us here in Amsterdam."
"To tell you the truth, Olga, I can't completely answer your question right now. What I can say is that it is true that I will maybe go to America to work there regularly. I just don't know all the details yet.
I can also tell you that my plan is to keep our office here open and to make you a managing director of RW Records."
Cream – "W.O.O.W" appeared playing in the room.

Olga smiled as he gave her the last bit of news. He had been looking forward to seeing the look on Olga's face.

"You can't be serious!"

Her face registered disbelief.

"I am indeed serious; please not mention it to anyone else for the moment."

Olga appeared in shock and could manage only to sit down in her chair. She automatically picked up the phone and called her sister.

At two o'clock Mono showed up back in the office as promised. To his surprise, he happened to be the only one present.

But then Mono saw that Olga left a note on his desk saying she had to go for family reasons.

He sat down to check his email, and after a minute, he had an idea. He picked up the telephone and dialed Daniel's number.

"Hi Daniel,"

"Where are you? I thought you were in L.A."

"I'm right here in Amsterdam, man. Listen, can we get together?"

"Always straight to the point when do you have in mind?"

"Now," Mono answered quickly. "The thing is, my schedule has gotten totally crazy, and now I am in a huge hurry."

The Visions of Shiva - "How Much Can You Take" - Original Mix occurred playing in the office.
"Alright, come on over. It is great timing because you can check out the footage for Tabitha's video clip."
"Great! I will be there in ten minutes."
Mono hung up the phone and Jo walked into the office.
"I cannot believe you are already back here."
"Yeah, Jo, it's true. And I am on my way out again. Listen, tomorrow I will be with The Funky Fakirs in the studio all day so please, no calls."
Joe confirmed the request.
Mono went on.
"Do you have any news on pre-orders from Free Record stores?"
"They confirmed 100 copies each release for now."
"Good Job Jo this is a promising start."
Mono rushed out of his office.

Daniel immediately began to organize the tapes of Tabitha performance from the fashion show.
He knew his friend want him to be prepared, to get right down to business.
Just as he found the last tape, the doorbell rang.
"Mono!", "The door is open. Please come in."
They exchanged a little bit of friendly small talk.
Daniel teased, "Appeared you actually in Los Angeles or acted it just a big joke?"

"No, man, I stayed there, but only for five days. I planned on a longer stay, but some important business changed my plans."
"Okay, tell me what I can do for you."
It emerged Daniel's turn to get down to business.
"Daniel, the main reason I called you, I want to see the footage. I have some ideas for additional scenes in my mind, but first I need to see what we already have."
Both watched selected scenes of footage from the fashion show at the Escape Club.
Mono acted staring at the screen in concentration, and he didn't say a word the entire time. Daniel watched him for a little while until he finally broke the silence.
"So, what do you think?"
"I guess that's okay for now, though. We will have two more shootings, and we should be able to put together a decent clip. The goal is to get rotation on Dutch music television. And our work is what I had hoped for, so I am satisfied so far."
Daniel listened and nodded. As usual, Mono seemed firm but honest. At least he appeared happy for the moment.
"In the meantime, Daniel, have you put any thought into other locations?"

Daniel had a big smile on his face because he had been expecting that exact question. "Of course I have like I promised. There is a casino in Zandvoort that is, in my opinion, a very great location. It has two floors with high ceilings, and the architecture is outer spacious, especially with all of the gambling machines in the background. I think we can shoot some great scenes there."
"I agree, Daniel that sounds fascinating. Should I check out the place?"
"If you would like, I can arrange something for you. But I am sure you will like it."
"Okay, I will take your word for it. We will shoot there. Do you have any other locations in your mind?"
"I kept thinking maybe Amsterdam, in the daytime, on a boat driving down the canals."
"Honestly, Daniel, I continued thinking about the same thing. Having some of the city in the clip would be nice. But something came up. In little time, Tabitha will perform at the Palace Club in Paris. I will talk to the producer of the show, and maybe we can record the show. In the daytime, we can shoot some scenes in the streets of Paris."
"If you could make that happen, you would be a genius! And I promise I will do everything in my power to keep the budget as low as possible."
Daniel remained to learn fast how to please him.
"That is something that I love to hear. But there is one more important thing. We can't waste any time because I am leaving for Brazil and everything has to be ready before I go. I need you to try to arrange it so that we can shoot in Zandvoort as soon as possible, maybe even this week."

"You want this week already?" Daniel made no attempt to hide his feelings. Mono kept asking for a lot from him this time. "This is a very short notice. My cameraman works for MTV, and I have no idea if he will be available so soon. Alright, look, let me first call the location. Even better, I will drive by today. I will make some phone calls later, and by tomorrow evening you will have the schedule in your email. "Daniel, this sounds like a plan to me."

V

Magic Inspiration

On the way back to his house, Mono relished the walk across Leidse Square. The lively square occurred to be the heart of Amsterdam, filled with fine stores, diverse restaurants, and tourists from all around the world. He invariably stopped to watch something, be it an artist's performance, a street football match, or a group of small children playing some obscure games. On this particular walk, he found himself staring only at the gray sky. He acted abnormally distracted because once again Faith's smiling face had come into his brain. He knew it had nothing to do with their work together and he just couldn't make sense of it. When Mono finally arrived at the front door of his house, he appeared still deep in thoughts. He decided to bypass the office and walked straight up the narrow staircase to his apartment.

Tabitha kept already waiting, and he could see the melancholy in her eyes. He could easily predict the first words from her lips.

"What's up?" she whined. "You don't have time for me anymore?"

Trying to calm her down, Mono cooed, "Tabitha, please, let us sit down, drink coffee, and talk about the little bit about the future."

He pulled two chairs up to the small table by the bed. Mono offered a seat to Tabitha, but she did go already to the kitchen.

"I have a pot of hot tea here, "Is this good enough for you?"

"Sure, babe, that would be perfect."

Tabitha walked over to the table and poured two cups of tea while he sat down in the chair and stretched his legs. "I want to thank you for your commitment and great work you did for our project. But look, Tabitha, my whole company, is working on your career at the moment. Our efforts just got you into the next issue of Elle magazine."

"Yes, Mies, of course, I know all of it, and I do appreciate it. But I only want to be with you, and for me, that is the most important thing."

"But you are with me all of the time."

And he asked her nicely for another cup of tea.

Tabitha stood up and poured another drink, but she didn't lose track of the conversation.

"No, I'm not," she said sadly. "And you know it. Most of the time I am alone in this goddamn house while you are traveling in some far away country, far away from me."

Tabitha kept slowly testing the patience. Mono would not tolerate these kinds of petty complaints from anyone.

"You are living like a princess with me. I mean, you have a maid who does everything for you. You can come and go as you please always. You are staying in a beautiful house, and the only thing that you have to do, take care of your mind and your body. I have to do my job. I cannot stay in one place with you for twenty-four hours. I love you, Tabitha. Your demands are just impossible. So please, baby, don't play these childish games with me anymore. You are twenty years old, but you have experienced a lot already."
Mono didn't get a chance to finish his last sentence before Tabitha began to scream.
"Mies, I hate you! All these girls are always around you, and it is making me crazy."
He couldn't keep his voice down anymore, and he joined her screaming.
"Which girls please?" Mono appeared angry. "You are silly, babe!"
She had pushed him too far with her last comment, and he jumped up from the chair.
He despised when someone questioned his integrity.
"You know I can't stand these kinds of conversations. If you want to change something, let me know."
Tabitha looked at Mono's angry face and did not say a word. Before he could see her cry, she walked out of the room and straight down to the front door.
Mono watched her from above when she kept walking in direction Utrecht Street. She stayed talking on her cell phone as a car stopped next to her. Tabitha opened the passenger door, stepped into the car and disappeared into the night.

Gino and Max appeared to walk towards the studio when Gino noticed Mono's car already parked in a visitor spot. He pointed it out to Max, who acted not at all surprised.

"Of course, man. Mono wants to make sure that everything is perfect this time."

Bass Studios nestled near the Amstel River port side close the heart of Amsterdam. The owner occurred to be a very ambitious and intelligent young engineer. His professional skills emerged renowned all over Europe.

The Funky Fakirs entered the studio and saw Mono already absorbed in conversation with Bass.

The producers' acted so engrossed in their conversation that neither of them heard The Funky Fakirs comes into the room. After a few seconds, both realized they stayed no longer alone. Bass acted the first to talk.

"Hi, guys!" Bass greeted them. He seized them by the hands and pulled them further into the room. "Come on; I want to show you around my studio. As you know, we don't have any time to waste here."

Mono jumped up and embraced both The Funky Fakirs in one big hug.

"What's going on guys?" Without waiting for an answer, Mono continued to talk excitedly.

"Alright guys, let's do it! But listen up, after our recording session here, we need to sit down for a little while and talk about the CDs. A few things have changed in our plan."

Max looked at Gino and shot him a look as if to say, "I told you so."

"I knew this afternoon wouldn't be our last session."
Max words made Mono smile.
In the early hours of the following morning, the air in the small studio happened to be thick with cigarette smoke. Out of the speakers came a stream of trance sounds from the future "Hot Weekend Amsterdam" records.
Mono asked Bass to turn down the music. "So, guys, what do you think of your work so far?"
Gino answered for both of them.
"Well, I think we did a good job, but to tell you the truth, after sixteen hours of work I need to catch some sleep and after listen to it again. But the most important thing," with an expectant smile, "is what do you think?"
"Yeah," Max jumped in, "what do you believe?"
Bass acted watching the dialogue from in front of the mixing board, and he smiled when he heard Max's predictable question.
Mono took the issue seriously, however, and he gave them a well-thought out answer.
"That is an amusing question, Max. It's like asking a man who just bought a car two hours ago, about the qualities of the vehicle so far.
First of all, you know that I love our playlist. I like your interpretation of the songs, good mixes. You guys made a great sequence here, and for sure I have to give you credit for this. I am happy with it."
The Funky Fakirs acted satisfied with his answer.
They knew better than to expect a standing ovation from him at this point in the game.
But Mono seemed not finished talking yet.

"Guys, I told you that I had a little news. Well, now I can say to you. The work we just did materialize going to be for promotional records."
Mono had just dropped a bomb, and the guys acted stunned, not sure how to react or whether or not to take him seriously.
Gino finally managed to ask, "Are you kidding?"
"No, man, I never joke about these kinds of things. You guys are going to have to trust me here. Our goal with this double album is to get a distribution deal with ID&T. So I needed these two CDs as promo samples.
The only reason I waited until now to tell you remained to make sure; I would get your full attention."
Gino and Max nodded, but they acted still not entirely convinced. Even though Mono had considerably more experience, they couldn't help but feel tricked.
Mono could see it in their faces. "Plus, guys, I am going to make a song together with Commander Tom, and Tabitha."
"Is it the German DJ who remixed the "Is E.T. On X.T.C.?" hit?" Max asked smiling.
That's the guy. Anyway, you guys will bootleg the new song, and we will add the new mix to the "Hot Weekend Amsterdam" track list. We are shooting a video clip for our song, and you guys will be the stars. What do you think?"
Max screamed, "Yes! My dream come true, I will finally be an actor."
 "Come on, man," Gino teased him, "you are a too huge man, and you can't even fit into the TV screen."

Max acted offended and shot him a nasty look. "That's not funny man."
Bass appeared watching all the action in silence since Mono had already revealed his plans to him at the afternoon conversation. They all acted absorbed in a new topic of conversation when Bass finally asked, "When will you record the final version of the CDs?"
"No later than last week of April, and guys, it is important that you start to play these records at your gigs."
"Yeah ok no problem. Last weekend on my radio show I already played a bunch of these releases. We had more phone calls in the studio that night than ever before. Fucking everyone appeared calling to find out the names of the tracks." Gino answered for both of them.
The entire studio lit up from Mono's giant smile. "Guys, as long as we stay entirely focused on this album, everything will be alright. Let's pack our stuff and get out of here. I need to take a detour and visit a friend in Eindhoven."
Max made up his funny face and asked, "Are you visiting Wayne?"
"Yes, I will he has a mixtape from a new DJ for me. He refused to send it by mail to the office the other day."
Gino responded. "Will he take our job over in the future? What's his name?
 "Don't worry guys; I am not looking to replace you. Maybe you have heard of him; his name is DJ Tiesto."
Max had the answer first. "He is resident at Spock in Breda."

Mono made a surprised face. "You are the man; I did checking the place out with Sunni together a while ago. I remember the name. Anyway, I have to drive to Eindhoven. Thank you; it lasted a pleasure as always. I am leaving."

"Gino, it is all about the right timing."
"Max, come on, what the hell, seemed to be our conversation about timing? Just concentrate on the highway. I don't want to be a famous dead DJ. How many joints did you smoke already today?"
"Not one, man. You know Mono, no pot at work."
"Damn," Gino said, looking at the highway sign, "it's twenty kilometers until Amsterdam, and I am starving. That happened to be a marathon recording session."
Max nodded in agreement, but he didn't say anything for a few minutes because he kept trying to piece together a puzzle in his head.
"Gino," "why do you think Mono continues delaying our double album?"
"Why do you ask me these things, Max? You have known this dude a lot longer than me; Mono is your friend way more than mine."
"Yeah, but I haven't been in the business long enough to understand his moves."
"Only he knows, but Mono said: 'DJs will be stars at the coming century.' I can tell you that this guy is working vigorously to create something special.

But Max, come on, we will talk about this later. Just concentrate on the road! You keep crossing over the lines, and it is making me crazy. I don't want to eat my next meal in a hospital bed. Look, let me make only one last comment about it. I will for sure go all the way with the man."
"Yeah, my friend this is the plan."
Max appeared sick of hearing Gino's whining that he kept his gaze frozen on the highway the entire ride home. Mainx — 88 To the Piano — Original Mix beating in the car.

Mono woke up in his bedroom and wondered appeared yet another rainy day in Amsterdam? Like always, the night before he had closed his sliding door not a single ray of light could sneak into the bedroom. He rolled out of bed, opened the door and walked to the other side of the huge room to see through the curtains how the rain happened to pelt against the window. He thought about Tabitha for a fleeting second, but his stomach growled impatiently, so he threw on a jogging suit and headed towards the kitchen. Through his half-opened eyes, he saw that Janse appeared already waiting there, busily preparing some food.
Mono's coffee occurred already on the table.
Janse looked up from the cutting board and said, "You look terrible."

"Yes," he finished her sentence, "I know, and I am too skinny."
The sounds of X-Caps - "Adena" woke him up."
Janse shook her head in frustration. She wished he would take better care of himself. His hair stayed wild, and his clothes had apparently come from the pile at the foot of his bed.
Mono seemed not in the mood for the usual morning banter, and he decided to ignore his growling stomach. He filled his cup with coffee and went straight down to the office with only a quick goodbye to a frowning Janse.
Janse yelled down behind him that his dinner is already prepared and waiting, he needs only to pop it in the microwave.

"Mono, you look like shit."
"Olga, please, I already heard it from Janse this morning."
Mono walked straight to his desk. His worries about Tabitha combined with the rainstorm left him in a particularly unfriendly mood. He sat down and saw a note on his desk written in big block letters. "CALL FROM BRAZIL."
"Olga, what's this about?"

"Oh, sorry about my incomplete note I put on your desk. Some guy from Brazil called, but I couldn't understand a word of his English, so I gave him your email address. You should have a mail from him by now."
"Was the name, Thomas?"
"No, definitely not it sounded something like DJ Marky, but I don't know for sure."
Mono shrugged his shoulders and turned to the computer to check his inbox. Olga ignored his rudeness and continued talking.
"So how did everything go in the studio yesterday?"
Without looking up from the monitor, he gave a curt answer.
"Great play the tapes they are super cool."
They both worked listening to music until he finished checking his things.
"Olga, I didn't get anything from Brazil here," Mono continued.
"Listen, I left the CDs from yesterday on Jo's desk, please make sure he makes copies. And when you talk to him, tell him to step up the promotion for the records, we need to close with a distributor."
After that, he dropped a little surprise, "Mono style."
"There is one more thing, Olga. I need you to update the "Hot Weekend Amsterdam" one Sheet. Where it says 'track list,' write 'promotional track list' and change the release date to June 1st."
But his sneaky approach emerged not unsuccessful.

"Are you kidding?" "Olga, please, do I look like I am in the mood to make jokes right now? Those CDs we recorded yesterday are only promo samples. We will not have the final track list until the end of April maybe. Also, I need you to call the record labels and inform them of the change of release date." "Look, don't you understand that people are already calling and asking me about the albums? You have to let me know in advance when you make significant changes to it. I don't want to be bullshitting to people, and I don't want to look stupid. Did I miss something here?"

"No, not at all I just told you, right? I want to have the albums out at the end of the spring, and the track list is open again, I will put Tabitha's new song on CD one."

"Tabitha has a new song? I don't know anything about Tabitha's new song!"

"Yeah, Olga, well now you do. "I love the dance I do." Isn't this a good project name for Tabitha? It's ready to run."

It appeared not particularly comforting to Olga. She didn't like surprises and the morning had been one surprise after another.

"I can see that you aren't in the mood for my questions, but can you at least tell me why you changed the deadline?"

"Olga, I never did, after our failure with B.B.E. Tabitha staring is my plan b." Mono smiled. "I only want one thing. I want the best for our records."

"Okay, I see," Olga answered, with a hint of anger creeping into her voice. She had had enough of his games. "I know a little inside your head now."

Mono felt guilty because he acted taking out his frustrations unfairly. In truth, Mono did like to work with Olga.

"Look, Olga, this is obviously not my day. My body is not in the right balance. You have done enough work over the week, so please go home and enjoy your weekend. It's already Saturday almost noon."

"Thanks, but I can't," she grumbled, "I still have some things left to do."

Even with the computer, Mono seemed to have trouble. It took him ten minutes to send just one mail.

Olga ignored Mono's frustrated curses and stayed deeply focused on her work when Mono suddenly let out an excited scream.

"Wow!"

Olga looked up expectantly.

"Olga, I just got the email from that guy in Brazil. I got an offer to produce a show in Rio de Janeiro!"

"Wow, congratulations!" "Who wrote you the email?"

"The show appears to be sponsored by Radio Transamerica, and it looks like an exciting production."

Keeping with the pattern of the day, Mono hadn't answered her question.

"But, who sent you the offer? And why are they asking you?

"Hey! What is that supposed to mean?"

"I only meant that Brazil is far away from Amsterdam. Sorry, but you are not exactly Mikel P, you know?"
Mono had a pen in his hand, and he launched it across the room, hitting the wall behind Olga's head.
"I warned you," he teased. "One more time and you are out of the office."
Olga reached behind her back, grabbed a pillow, and launched a counter-attack.
Mono blocked the fluffy missile with his arms. Right after putting both hands up in the air. "I give up, you win. I will answer your question. The guy who sent the email said that we met through my friend Stephan Schuster at the "Love Parade" 1992 in Berlin. I am a recommendation of the investors of the event."
"Rio de Janeiro? Do you remember him?"
"Olga...., when I worked for both official "Love Parade" parties that year I must have met five hundred different people. I stayed permanently high on XTC haha. Super party times indeed. I maybe have little clue who the guy is. Right now I am going to think about it, and I will talk it over with Faith."
At the mention of Faith's name, a little spark came into Olga's eyes.
"You have been talking about her quite a bit these last few weeks."
Mono rolled his eyes at her little smirk.
"Faith called here last night, in case you didn't get the message."
"Yes, Olga, I know, we spoke in the middle of the evening. She also told me that you two talked for quite a while."
Now they both acted smirking.

"Oh, it is a girly thing. And Faith is a very sweet girl. Speaking of which, boss, I know you don't want my questions today, but what is going on with Miami? Faith tells me that you two will open an office there? Is this a plan? Why do you have all of these secrets lately?"

Dance 2 Trance - "Warrior" played beating in the room.

"Nothing at all seems sure; all of the plans are still up in the air."

"I have been working with you for a little while only, but I think I know your pattern a little. Are you guys working on a record in America?"

Mono slammed his agenda shut and jumped up from his desk.

"You know what, Olga? Don't forget our new interim is coming in on Monday after his school. Sebastian is his name." Olga took a deep breath. "I have it on my agenda, what I do with him?"

"Let him catalog all of the white label records and other promos; we received in the last three months. Let him spin our records; he can use our turntables in the basement as he wishes."

Mono appeared smiling. "My weekend just has begun one minute ago Olga. I will see you on Monday morning."

Mono walked towards the Palladium restaurant on Leidse Square, enjoying an unusually sunny Saturday afternoon. The dry, cold air seemed thoroughly refreshing. Tabitha walked alongside him until they came to the entrance of the square.
"Mies, I would rather go on my Saturday shopping trip. I need some clothes for Paris. Could I go?" "OK, enjoy your afternoon. We don't need you around anyway. Give me a kiss."
She ducked into the taxi. "I won't be back at home before five, Tabitha. Have fun today!"
Mono's thoughts immediately turned to his lovely chicken salad at the Palladium.
Daniel arrived already sitting at a table directly behind the door. Daniel saw him walk in and caught his attention by waving a yellow napkin in the air.
"I already ordered you a cappuccino."
"Great," Mono grinned, and they shook hands across the table.
Mono hung his jacket on the back of the chair and sat down with a smile. Without saying a word, he took a long look around the restaurant, appreciating the ambiance and checking out the clientele. The Palladium always crowded with Amsterdam's upper class along with tourists. Mono loved the restaurant for both the food and the decor. The colors of the walls designed peaceful and relaxing, and the chicken salad seemed out of this world.
Daniel responded watching his unusual movements.
"Are you looking for someone?" "No," he answered with a calm voice, smiling.
I am just enjoying my surroundings on this pleasant afternoon."

The waiter brought over two cappuccinos and after noted down on a paper Mono's new order.
"So, where is Tabitha today?"
"She planned going to join us, but she went on her shopping tour instead."
"Oh, that's a shame. Please give Tabitha my greetings. Look, I apologize that we couldn't do the shoot this week. But, you gave me such short notice that there emerged little I could do. My cameraman just couldn't make it. But tomorrow night, as soon as the casino closes down, we can start to shoot and have eight hours to film our scenes."
"You think that is enough time?"
"Yes, I am sure it is."
Daniel pulled a thin pile of papers out of his briefcase and handed them to him.
"Here, look at this. I sketched the scenes for you."
Mono took the papers and carefully checked through the scenes for a while. "We need more scenes."
"Did you speak with the dancers?"
"Oh, you know how those guys are always impossible to reach. But I talked with Kenny, and he promised me that he would talk to Vince. And Kenny already sent me an email confirming the date and the time for the shoot. So those guys know exactly when and where they have to be in Zandvoort. They got this booking from Toffy so believe me; they will not fuck it up. It is an excellent opportunity for them."
Mono acted somewhat nervous to hear that Daniel hadn't spoken with Vincent and he reacted not quite as convinced as Daniel that there existed nothing to worry about today. Mono pushed the matter when Daniel interrupted his thoughts.

"Maybe I shouldn't be asking you, but I am curious, what is going on with Tabitha? I spoke with her on the phone yesterday, and she sounded kind of weird."
"Daniel, come on man that is none of your business. I will take care of Tabitha. She is just nervous, like always. I mean, her entire life has changed in the past six months, and she just needs to get used to this business.

We have more important things to discuss this afternoon. Did you see my mail about Paris?"
Daniel acted a little embarrassed and happy to move to another topic of conversation.
"Yes, I am thrilled to hear that the work in Paris will happen. As far as the travel arrangements, everything is already taken care of."
"Wait for a second, Daniel; I already knew that. Wow, man, sometimes I think I am getting old. Olga left me your message in a note on my desk. Sorry about that."
That seemed a strange moment for both of them. Mono rarely slipped up in business conversations, and they both knew it.
Mono cleared his throat and paused before speaking again.

"Anyway, Daniel, our whole schedule in Paris is going to be very fucking tight. Kenny and Vincent are coming to Paris straight from a show in Germany. Both will have a twelve hours window and fly straight back to Germany. The thing is, their plane leaves Paris at six in the morning, and Tabitha's performance at the Palace is scheduled for three am. Can you see why I am a little bit nervous about our whole job?" Mono Stretched his chin. "I want you to know you have done a great job so far and I appreciate your help in general."
Mono looked up as a visitor arrives. "As we speaking of the devil."
"Am I?" "Happy to see you today, Mono."
"It is good to see you again Peter. How are you?
Peter tried to bring a huge smile on his face.
"I am good. Tabitha told me where I could find you. I met her at Hooftstraat. I want to talk to you about your offer; it has been running through my mind for a while now." Mono managed to mask his surprise and politely introduced Daniel to Peter. Mono opened his arms. "Feel free to talk Peter." Peter acted searching for the right opening. "I like your project. We will power it. I will mix one of your upcoming albums. Take a CD-R with my logo please." Peter handed a CD to a surprised Mono and went on. "I would like to discuss details with you." Mono smiled. "Nice to hear that, we can sit down anytime you want and talk about it again." Peter needed a second to come with a proper response. "I will come Monday afternoon to your office. How sounds this for you?" "It's sound perfect to me." Peter and Mono shook hands. Peter departed wishing both an excellent weekend.

Daniel couldn't hold a surprised face. Mono silenced him. "Let's go over the scenes one more time."

Mono's packed schedule necessitated a rare Saturday evening in the office. Shuffling through the endless paperwork, he worked enjoying the silence until the telephone rang. Curious, Mono first checked the caller ID screen and saw it was an Amsterdam number. Usually, he wouldn't pick up a phone call at that hour, but he recognized Phil's code. Phil, the Dutch writer, occurred to be a good friend, and it would be fun to have a little small talk with him.
He picked up the phone and said, "Hi Phil, long time no talk."
Phil acted startled, as he had predicted.
"How did you know it's me, man? Are you a magician now?"
"No Phil, it's just a little high technology in action. So what's going on with you, man? How the hell could you possibly know I would be in my office on a Saturday night?"
"Well, I saw Tabitha this afternoon at the shopping mall Magna Plaza. She did telling me how crazy your schedule is these days, so I gave it a shot."
Mono found it amusing how quickly information travel in this small village sometimes.
 "Anyway," Phil continued, "I just wanted to thank you."

"Thank me? You are the one who wrote the lyrics for "Where is My Love?" I should be thanking you, man."
"Yeah, well the guys at Magic Trax just asked me to give singing lessons to some of the girls over there. It is some money that I can use right now. And I know that the reason they asked me because you remained talking good about my work to everyone."
"Phil, man, give you a little bit of credit here. They asked you because they have seen your skills. I mean, Tabitha wouldn't be able to sing a note without your many lessons. So I appreciate the gesture but please, Phil, don't thank me. However, I must admit I am a little bit curious here. To whom will you be giving these singing lessons over there?"
Phil had just been waiting for the chance to tell him the names of his new students. He seemed sure he would appreciate the "coincidence." Phil explained to him that he would soon be giving singing lessons to both Wendy and Harold's girlfriends.
"Phil," he howled, "that is absolutely some awesome stuff. Thanks for the news, man!" He went on. "That's fabulous."
His reaction repeated what Phil had expected.
"But seriously," Mono continued, "I have something else what may interest you. Tomorrow night we are recording some scenes for the 'Where is My Love' video clip. Why don't you stop by and check out the shoot? Robby can come by and pick you up in the evening.
I will call you tomorrow afternoon with the exact time."
"That would be great. Thank you."
"Don't worry about it; I know you are a good guy."

"Mies, do you like my new outfit?" Dance 2 Trance - "We came in Peace" kept streaming from the CD player. He walked into the barely-lit room and could see a porn movie playing on the television.
"Wow, Tabitha," he said, "I love it. It's fucking hot."
"Yeah," she whispered. "And I am very excited too." Tabitha sat down on the living room table and opened her legs. Mono saw her glistening pussy. Mono moved closer and saw how she appeared penetrating herself with a vibrator to his surprise.
"It's just for you, Mies," she cooed. "It's for our pre-video shoot sex."
She began screaming and pushed the vibrator very deep into her wet pussy; she could not hold it anymore and exploded into a long, intense orgasm. Mono appeared watching the scene and before Mono realized the happenings; Tabitha had his dick in her mouth and brought it up and down through her lips. She acted still very horny and pushed him down, so she could lick his penis and in the same time pierce her pussy, by thrusting herself onto his leg. They both exploded only after seconds.

The casino in Zandvoort transformed from a crowded gambling hall into a microcosm of a Hollywood movie set. Crewmembers laden with cameras and lights had invaded the ornate vestibule and centered on the spiraling descent of a red-carpeted staircase.

Daniel acted clearly in charge and loudly directed each of the scenes. After yelling, "Cut!" he peered into the tiny TV monitor alongside himself and the cameraman.

"What do believe?"

"I want to see this scene one more time."

Bob, the cameraman, rewound the tape and they all watched the scene again.

"Look, Bob," he pointed at the monitor, "you see how she is walking down the stairs here? She isn't paying attention to the camera."

"Yeah you're right," Bob said, "I can film the next time better."

Daniel called Tabitha over to the monitor to show her the scene while he explained what he wanted.

"Tabitha, you have to walk down the stairs with a groove in your hips, look straight at the camera, and make a fucking horny face."

"How can I make a sensual look?" she asked innocently.

Mono snorted. "Come on, Tabitha; just think about the last letter you sent me."

Tabitha stuck out her tongue, but Daniel ignored the comment. He acted frustrated with Tabitha's inexperience.

"Tabitha, honey, you need to catch the viewers with your beautiful fucking face."

"I will try," she promised.

Daniel said a small prayer to himself and called the crew together once more.

In the meantime, Tabitha leaned her body against his and sighed deeply.

"Oh Mies," "I am already so exhausted and can't work anymore today."
"Just one more time, baby, and we will be ready to go home."
"You said that already one hour ago!" she cried. "I don't think that you and Daniel will ever be satisfied."
"Come on, baby," he pleaded, "let's do it one more time."
He yelled to the tone engineer to play the music.
The crew worked for one more hour until all acted finally satisfied. Tabitha seemed destroyed and sprawled out on a chair in the casino restaurant. She sat next to Kenny and Vincent the Suriname dancers and they were all relieved to see the cleaning women arrive. The shoot appeared over.
Bob told Daniel the footage seems excellent. Mono agreed, and the rest of the crew acted too tired to utter any objections.
"Guys," yelled out to the team, "I know everyone here is exhausted and that you all want to get the hell out of here. Just give me one more chance to watch that scene again where Kenny and Vince do the back flips."
They groaned in unison, but Mono got his final wish.
"Alright guys," Thank you so much, you all did a great job tonight." The whole crew appeared clapping hands and screaming. "Paris we are coming!"

VI

Pleasure Zone

Thin rays of sunlight pierced the curtains in Faith's big bedroom, drawing yellow stripes on her bare legs. She remained asleep and laid out over half of her huge bed when the blaring alarm clock jerked her awake. It appeared to be nine in the morning, Miami time.

She opened one eye and saw the statistic sheets still spread out over the empty half of the huge bed. She had been working the entire night until she eventually fell asleep on top of the piles of papers. Still completely exhausted, Faith willed her eyes open. Suddenly his face popped into her head. It occurred to be already in the middle of the afternoon in Amsterdam, so she decided to give Mono a call. After dialing the number for his cell phone, she heard some fumbling on the other end of the line and following an unintelligible greeting.

"Where are you?" Her voice cracked as she said her first words of the day.

"Good morning Faith. To tell you the truth, I'm still in bed. We finished shooting the video clip in Zandvoort last night until eight in the morning."

"I'm sorry," she apologized, "I completely forgot. Do you want me to call you back later?"

"No, no, it's fine. I need to wake up now anyway."

"Okay, good morning! I just woke up too by the way. I called to give you an update on my progress these last few days. Tell me first how the shooting went."

"I guess it emerged okay," "I mean, shooting a music video is an interesting thing for me, you know? I just hope all of our efforts will pay off. Next weekend we are filming the final scenes in Paris, and that should be again exciting. Hey, you know what? Why don't you fly over to Paris and join us? I would love to see you."

"I honestly wish I could. You know what my schedule is like, though."

She acted a little surprised at the offer and even more surprised at how her stomach dropped in response. Maybe she just needed to get some breakfast.

"So," she continued, ignoring her stomach, "now for the news from Miami. The thing, which happened to be my main reason for calling, I made contact with a bunch of distributors, stores on the east and west coast I introduced myself as a researcher. I got some very satisfying answers to my questions."

"It's pleasing news."

"Yes, I am great with our progress. There exist more I want to discuss; I already sent you a mail about all issues. I know you are busy, but please try and answer by today or tomorrow. You mentioned something about producing a show in Brazil, but I couldn't understand what you meant."

"Sorry," Mono apologized, "as always it is my bad - English. Let me explain. We got an offer to produce a show in Rio. Anyway, the show seems scheduled for the end of April."

"And we are going to do it?" Faith asked, sounding surprised.
"I'm not sure yet but definitely should considering it."
"You would stay in Rio de Janeiro for several weeks?"
"No, that is not possible. I am still thinking about how we can fit this into our schedule. When we are in Brazil, I will have a meeting with these guys, after we make our decision. But Faith, since we are on the phone now, why don't you go ahead with your issues? Do you want me to call you back first?"
"It's okay; I have one of those special telephone cards, so I'm only paying a few cents a minute. It turned out my statistic requests mobilized a music visionary. I need a pre-production start date for our American trance project, and I need it no later than Thursday morning, Eastern Time. I promised it to Galgano. He called the office yesterday."
Mono appeared walking with the cell phone in his hand in the direction to the diner room window. He liked watching the beautiful Weteringsschans Street for a second from above after he woke up.
"We can't have a date for another four weeks, not until after our meeting in Sao Paulo. I guess even much later. We are in a very early stage with it. We will need for development in Amsterdam 9 months more minimum time figure. I will answer your email as best as I can. But we need to bullshit a little bit. You need to buy a lot of time. I know how important Galgano could be for our plan."
"Let me think how we can handle this situation. I will come up with something and talk with Galgano."
Mono had enough business talk for the moment, so he asked her about life in Miami.

"What did you do this weekend?"

"Wow, it ended up being a pretty hectic week. As always, I had dinner with my mom on Friday and breakfast with my dad on Saturday. I missed Bagel Cove like crazy, and I devoured a huge plate of lox and cream cheese. Friday night I turned a little tired, I met Dawn and DJ Lex at Billabong for some pitchers of Newcastle."

"How are they doing?" He interrupted.

"They are doing great as always. We laughed all night, catching up on the past few months. And of course, they both send you greetings. Anyway, Saturday night I motivated a little bit and headed down to South Beach with Sandy and some guys from high school. You should see the beach these days; everything is all hip hop. Finally, at four in the morning, we left the beach and headed downtown to Club Space. Downtown Miami has changed so much in the last few years. There are three after hour clubs on the 11th street alone, and you wouldn't believe all of the construction near the American Airlines Arena. Club Space packed like always, and we didn't get home until 10 am. Somehow I made it out for the last hour of sundown at the pool and after I spent the entire evening in my apartment, catching up with all this paperwork."

She paused for a moment, and he jumped in.

"How is your mom doing?"

"Good, thanks for asking. I am meeting Mom for lunch at Giorgio's this afternoon."

"Oh, nice please say hi to her for me."

 Jo stayed alone at the office, looking over some contract proposals. After reading the same sentence three times, he threw down the papers in frustration. Jo appeared a confident guy typically and could always keep his cool under pressure, especially at work. Only in the past few days had he began to feel an unusual amount of stress. Work had become so overwhelming that Jo started questioning his decision to leave university for the job at RW Records. He tugged at his tight blond ponytail and reflected over his predicament until Mono came into the office and interrupted the daydream.
Pushing the negative thoughts from his mind, Jo smiled and greeted his boss.
"Robby just called, he wants to know what time you are leaving for Paris on Friday morning."
"Did you tell him I would call him back?"
"No," Jo answered, "I said you would be busy all day and I would call him later with a reply."
"Thanks. Tell Robby that we will be leaving at six in the morning on Friday. But tell him he should try and get to Amsterdam by Thursday evening so we can be sure to get out of Amsterdam on time. And Jo, please call Daniel for me? I need you to give him the message we are meeting in Paris at 12:30 at the Carlton Hotel. And lastly," he said on his way out the door, "If anyone needs me, only for an emergency, you can reach me on my cell phone."
Mono seemed backing out of the door when he bumped into Olga as she walked in the office.
"Oh hey, I'm glad I caught you here. Listen, you need to call Nakka D, he has already called here two times today."

He asked her why she hadn't left him a note with the messages. Olga walked straight to his desk, took a piece of paper off the place, and triumphantly waved it in the air.
"See? I did put a note on your desk."
He flashed a weak smile and apologized.
"Sorry, Olga, my fault, I should know you better. I am fucking lame. I will call him right now." He dialed Nakka D's number even though he only had time for a quick conversation. Nakka said hello, he got straight to the point.
"Nakka D, what's up brother? I'm sorry to rush you, but I'm in a hurry. What's wrong?"
"Nothing is wrong. I'm sorry for bothering you because I know how busy you are these days. I just have a quick favor to ask you. I have a cousin who lives in Spain, and he is just starting out as a DJ. He keeps telling me that he wants to play at a good club in Amsterdam I thought maybe you could do something for him. In my opinion, he has a lot of talent, and he is very young, so he has a lot of potentials. Maybe you can help him get his feet in the door."
"Okay, Nakka D, I get the point. Is he Spanish?"
"No, he lives in Barcelona, but he's Dutch."
"Okay, and what's his DJ name?" DJ Ruff," Nakka D answered "Man, that's a cool name. I tell you what, Nakka, drop off his tape at my office later, and I promise I will give it a listen. If I believe he has potential, I could help him out maybe. But please, bring it by soon because I am leaving for Brazil and I don't know about my schedule after."
"Great, thanks. It is very cool."

"Brother, you are always welcome."
Mono hung up the phone, said goodbye to Olga and Jo, and rushed out of the office.

Mono stepped into a taxi and gave the driver directions to Magic Studio. His voice acted cheerfully, and he had a wonderful feeling inside because everything appeared to be moving along as planned. He and Raul both arrived at the studio at the same time and, like always, they greeted each other with friendly hugs. Everyone with whom both worked could clearly see their mutual respect for one another.
"Hey, Raul," "are you in the mood to do some great things today?"
"Well," he said with enthusiasm, "I am one hundred percent ready as far as the computers and equipment. But the inspiration is your responsibility this afternoon. Today is the day you want to produce the song in memory of your friend right?"
"Yes, that's what I have in mind for this afternoon. They stood around the conference table and talked for a few minutes before entering the recording cabin. "So tell me, Raul, what are Eric and the other guys doing? You know," Phil described how he is giving singing lessons to Wendy and Harold's girlfriend.

Mono seemed enjoyable repeating the question and expecting a response. But Raul didn't notice it and instead explained to him. "You know, everybody here at the studio seems excited about your music project. I'm not sure if someone told you already, but when Tabitha performed on television, the studio happened to stay packed, and we all appeared watching the show. And now everyone is eagerly awaiting the clip." Mono heard the news for the very first time and felt overwhelmed.
"Wow, Raul that is very nice to hear.
This weekend we will be in Paris to record the final scenes of the video. And by the way, I noticed on the flyer that Eric will also be spinning at this show in Paris.
"I do not know Eric's DJ schedule honestly."
"Let's get started with the song now. I need to get these beats out of my brain and onto the tape where they belong."

They spent the rest of the afternoon and half of that evening inside the recording cabin. The session began undisturbed except for a short visit from Max and DJ D-Fact.
The small disturbance served a purpose, however, because they threw a few good ideas into the production.

Later in the evening, after listening to the finished
song for a felt tenth time, Mono still could not decide
his mood about it.
Raul watched the indecision on his face, so he asked
him straight out.
"And what are you thinking?"
He sat in silence until the indecision finally faded
from his face.
"Well, Raul," he said slowly, "I am sure. Our song
sounds good to me. It's up and down and again; it's
cool.
So now the rest of the work is for you. I need you to
have the master ready by next Wednesday."
"No problem."
Mono knew he would get what he needed when
promised by Raul. It had been a fruitful and fulfilling
studio session.

Mono asked Raul, "Let's check the studio booking log
for a second.
I want to see if there is a spot available at the
beginning of March."
"The book is over there on the desk," Raul pointed,
"the black one in the middle."
He flipped through the pages, but he couldn't
decipher the codes written inside.
"Raul, please take a look at this and tell me if there is
any time free at the beginning of the month."

Raul took the book in his hands and showed him where there appeared some space on the schedule. "You see here? You can have three days in a row. But can I ask what you want to do?"

"Of course, you can, Raul. I want to produce a trance song, to put on the "Hot Weekend Amsterdam" albums."

Raul didn't try to hide the incredulity in his face or his voice.

"You are going to promote trance albums in Holland?"

"Yes, I want. We have a plan".

"You know," Raul said, his voice now more relaxed, "Harold and Eric will be euphoric to hear you want to produce another song in our studio."

"You know what? I only want to do the pre - production here at Magic.

Anyway, it's getting kind of late; we should wrap things up. I will leave and let you close up everything here."

Mono packed up his briefcase and slung the strap over his shoulder. Mono had one more question before he acted ready to leave.

"Raul, by the way, how is Peter doing with his Earth, Wind, and Fire remake?"

"Well," Raul answered hesitantly, "we are working on some things. But you know Peter; he can be so challenging and domineering in the studio. The song seems work in progress. They have decided that the song working title it's about the word spontaneous, more I don't know. Peter and Eric still don't know if they will get the clearance they need from the Earth, Wind, and Fire label."

Mono said it sounded absorbing and that he remained sure it would be a success.

"I guess so," Raul said. "I hope so. But please, this time it's my turn to say that this is not for public discussion."

He gave him thumbs-up and said goodbye. Mono walked out smiling, just as he had walked in eight hours earlier.

One hour before the meeting time, Tabitha, Robby, and Mono acted busy at the reception, checking into the Carlton Hotel. All quickly went through the formalities and headed upstairs to drop off all bags and freshen up.

Mono had just finished a quick shower when Daniel knocked on his door. Daniel stopped by to tell Mono that the rest of the crew had arrived and everyone is relaxing.

"What time do you think we will get to work?" Daniel asked.

"Tell everyone we meet in the lobby ninety minutes from now. But Daniel, I need you to be there thirty minutes earlier. I want to talk with you about the scenes before we get started."

Sixty minutes later, Mono strolled down to the hotel lobby and found Daniel already waiting with two cappuccinos perched on the round table in front of him.

"Oh, Daniel, I just love how you are always thinking about me."

Daniel smiled but got right down to work, handing him a few papers over.

"Here are the scenes for today. I sketched everything down for you."

"Thanks, Daniel," he answered, "but it's not necessary right now."

Mono took a big gulp of coffee and savored the sweet flavor of his first Paris cappuccino in nine months. After swallowing, he recollected his thoughts.

"Yesterday I had some time off, and I spent a few hours looking over the footage we've already gotten. My opinion is that everything we have up until now is in a kind of equilibrium with the state of the song. What I am trying to say is that this whole production seems in the balance."

Daniel didn't like what he began hearing and interrupted him, sounding offended.

"Are you telling me you are not satisfied?"

"No, absolutely not, Daniel, don't worry. I am trying to explain how my wishes and my expectations are on target so far."

"What is that supposed to mean?" Daniel asked suspiciously.

"Look, Daniel, it has to do something with the whole purpose of the song, and it shouldn't bother you. I am sorry, but this is too complicated to explain right now, and it is not necessary. However, I can assure you that I am completely satisfied with your creative work."

Daniel did not look particularly convinced, but he ignored it for the time being and listened to Mono, what he said about new ideas for the filming.

"I don't know which scenes you planned for the afternoon, but I am going to tell you what I need. I want three street scenes; one of them on the Champs-Elysees, one on a crowded shopping street, and the last directly in front of the Eiffel Tower. And maybe, if we have enough time, I want one scene nearby the Seine.

I want to see Tabitha, Kenny, and Vincent in all of our scenes, looking for something, and I want happiness visible from our cast. We need to reflect the movement and the beauty of Paris in everyone's faces and gestures."

Mono finally paused for breath; Daniel had a chance to respond to his ideas. Daniel acted grinning with self-satisfaction.

"I had similar ideas in my mind. What about The Palace show?" "Daniel," Mono said excitedly, "all seem good! Concerning Tabitha's show tonight I will take care of the perfect sound, and we stick with your ideas for the filming."

Daniel handed him a piece of paper over. Mono accepted it and put the page folded in his jacket pocket.

Both very absorbed in the discussion that neither of them noticed how quickly time had passed. The cappuccinos stayed already cold, and the entire crew appeared waiting on the other side of the hotel lobby.

Robby, the Belgian driver, occurred to be elated, to have the Sunday evening Paris traffic behind him finally. He cruised at 120 miles per hour towards the France-Belgium border in his silver Mercedes 300E. Mono appeared in the passenger seat chatting away while Tabitha slept in the back seat.
 "Look," Robby pointed behind his head, "Tabitha is sleeping back there like a baby."
Mono leaned forward and turned up the stereo anyway.
Tabitha had been out cold since they left the Palace club and he seemed sure that not even a bomb would wake her up for another hour or two.
Both quietly tapped hands to the interesting beat.
"Why are we listening to it?" Robby asked. "It's good house music, but you have been playing the tape forwards and backward ever since we left Amsterdam on Friday morning."
"Tell me what you think about it," suggested his response.
When Mono acted mulling over a new idea, his tone of voice inspired a particular curiosity. "Why are you asking?"

"Robby, please, I will answer your question but can you first slow down a little bit, please? It is not a Formula one race here, and I don't feel like paying any speeding tickets for you back to your question. The tape appeared recorded to be by a talented young Dutch guy; his name selected is DJ Ruff. You remember Nakka D, right?"
"Yeah, of course," Robby laughed.
"Well, Nakka D asked me to do him a favor and get his cousin a gig in Amsterdam. DJ Ruff lives in Spain right now, but he has been trying to get some work in the Netherlands for a while."
"I think you should help him out," Robby said.
They drove past a big green highway sign, and the blue writing caught Robby's attention.
Robby perked up as an idea popped into his head.
"Hey! Let's stop in Ghent; it's already halfway to Amsterdam. I can give my mother a call. She will cook us a delicious dinner, and after we can relax a while at my parent's house. It seems we are already ahead of schedule, and we will still get to Amsterdam by midnight."
Mono already pictured the veal Milanese and Brussels sprouts steaming in butter and of course with the new potatoes.
Mono and Tabitha had been to Robby's parents' house several times before, and they had also been guests of his in Amsterdam. The house in Ghent seemed warm and cozy, and he couldn't imagine anywhere he would rather be at that moment.

"Robby," "I am in no hurry at all. I feel very relaxed now. Our first video clip is in post-production. I am excited about it. I would love to see your lovely parents and to have some dinner with them. It has been too long. And I am sure Tabitha will agree."

Olga and Mono appeared once again to work late at the office when the telephone rang suddenly.
"Please Olga," he said, without looking up from his papers, "can you take that call please?"
Olga said hello, and a look of surprise came across her face. "It's Vincent," she said, passing the phone to him.
She guessed he would want to take the call and his outstretched hand confirmed her assumption.
"Hi brother," Mono greeted him, "How's life treating you? Did you make it back in time for your show in Germany?"
"Oh yeah, we sure did. But it happened to be an adventure. First, the taxi driver in Paris drove us to the wrong airport, so we arrived at Charles de Gaulle thirty minutes late and missed the flight.
We had this gig at the "Fashion Week" in Germany, right? Working for a French designer and believe it or not, we ran into the owner of the company at the airport! So we all flew in his private jet to Düsseldorf, and we ended up making the show in time."

"But anyway," Vincent went on, without waiting for any reaction, "I am calling to find out when Daniel will finish the video clip. Do you have an idea?" Mono put the phone on speaker.

"Daniel told me Friday evening I can watch the final cut," are you so curious to see it?"

"I mean, of course, we are excited to see the video," Vincent explained. "I am asking. Do you know Anita, the member from 2 Unlimited?"

"Not personally," "but of course I know what she stands for."

"Well, Anita has her show now on TMF, Dutch music channel. I spoke with her about your new video clip. She asked me for Tabitha's video, to broadcast it as part of her program. Mono carefully considered his answer.

"Vincent, I need to think about it for a moment. But I will call you when I have a copy for you. Hopefully, it will be by Friday night or Saturday morning at the latest. Thanks for your help. I appreciate it. Give a hug and thank you to Anita and Kenny please."

Mono hung up the phone and watched in Olga's direction.

"Did I understand it right? Why you told Vincent that you have to think about it?"

He shook his head at Olga's over-eager reaction.

"I am very grateful for it. This opportunity will not disappear in the next two or three days. Of course, I want to get airplay for the clip. I need to see the final cut first. I mean, it is a lot at stake here. It's our first video production. Olga, let's develop this thing a little bit. I need to think about it."

"I see boss you smell a chance here."

He seemed to be scolding her, but Olga could see in his face that he acted euphoric with the news. She felt comfortable enough to push the matter a bit further.
"Just in case you decide to take the offer, when will the clip be on the show?"
"Olga," he said, feigning exasperation, "I have no clue, maybe in the middle of next month, perhaps even earlier."
Olga called her sister to tell her the news.

A little later mono appeared busy on his computer, doing some research on Yahoo. All of the sudden he interrupted the search as Olga walked close his desk.
"Olga," Mono said seriously, "I need you to do me a favor."
"Anything what can I do?"
"Please don't get on the phone and start calling everyone with the news. I want to keep this within the office for now. Nothing is sure right now."
He could see that Olga acted disappointed and it made him reconsider.
"You know what?" he said suddenly, "Fuck that. You can tell the whole world that the clip will be on television. But instead of TMF, tell everyone MTV. Okay? Keep in your mind the possibility it could be a lie anyway."
Mono watched Olga smiling. Olga liked it if Mono opened up her mind to a broader view of things.
As he had hoped, Olga no longer looked disappointed.

Instead, she acted puzzled. She asked if Mono could explain his odd request. He did not like to explain his business decisions to anyone, but Olga worked as one of his closest employees. He needed her trust.

"It's hard to explain, Olga," he began. "Let me put it this way. I know someone is trying to sabotage Tabitha's carrier. I have evidence. We nearly got screwed with the last TV gig, and I don't want to take any more risks."

He refused to elaborate any further. When he walked out the office five minutes later, Olga occurred left alone. She tried to be in his foot ones more again.

Mono appeared in his apartment, sitting in the dark. The only light emerged the glow from the television, which reflected off his glassy blue eyes. He acted deep in concentration and staring at the Sony TV screen. He watched the video clip for many times but still could not arrive at a final opinion about the work. For a moment he felt dizzy from the joint, he just smoked.

"What are you doing?"

Mono suddenly jumped to his feet when he heard the words spoken in his ear. Looking around, he saw that Sanni had been standing right next to his chair.

"Oh, Sanni I'm watching Tabitha's video clip. How did you get yourself into the house, brother?"

"I met Tabitha at the front door, and she let me in. I gave her some money to pick up some beers; I know you never have any here."
"I am happy you are here. I have the promo CD from the "Wagges" song at the player. Do you want to listen to it?"
"Sure I want to. Hold on a second, do I smell weed in here?"
"You have a good nose, Sanni. It is the hash from down the street. There is some on the table over there," he pointed, "roll us a joint if you like."
Both listened to the "Wagges" beats, smoking the large joint together. "What are you going to do with the track?"
"I am not done with the song yet, but I will put the Track on Tabitha's first vinyl."
"By the way," Sanni interrupted, "when did you last speak to Fuddle? I haven't been able to reach him for over a week now."
"You know Thomas Fuddler," Mono answered. "He lost his cell phone again. He seems using his girlfriend's phone. I have a number from Kim downstairs on my desk. Before we leave, remind me to get it for you. Anyway, back to my question. Do you like the song?"
"Of course, man, it is the "Wagges" song. He is grooving in time."
Cold beer thoughts broke the meditation.
"You know what man? I hope Tabitha didn't run into anyone outside because I want to drink a beer right now."

Sanni's wish came true. Tabitha walked right in with a bag full of beer.

After a short conversation with both, her eyes rested on the television screen. She saw the frozen image of her face and the excitement crept into her voice.

"Is that what I think it is?"

"Yeah, babe, I tried going to surprise you. Daniel finished editing, and he dropped off the tape a couple of hours ago."

He enjoyed watching Tabitha's excitement grow.

Sanni suggested a premiere presentation and opened three cans of beers in celebration.

"And you know what?" Sanni added, "I am also going to roll another joint."

"Not for me," Tabitha looked at the hash in disgust, "I absolutely can't stand that stuff. Give me candy, and I go for it."

Mono waited until the group had finished watching the video clip before dropping the news that would make her scream.

"Babe," he said slowly, "There are more things I haven't told you. We are going to get your video played on Anita's new show."

Sanni appeared the one to react to the news.

"Did you know that she sold millions of records around the world?"

"Yes," he answered. Mono could see Tabitha's arms shaking, but he seemed not finished yet talking about it.

"Anita has her show on TMF. It's called "Pleasure Zone," and she invited you to sing your song on her program. DJ Jean will be the star of the night. I confirmed the deal with Toffy, Kenny, and Vincent thirty minutes ago."
Now Tabitha acted completely freaking out.
"I cannot believe it! It is great!"
Sanni puffed on his new joint and watched her jump on top of him, planting kisses all over his face.
"Pleasure Zone is a good name," Sanni exhaled. "I've already heard about it. They broadcast every week from different dance clubs around the country. I am euphoric for you guys."
"I am very nervous. When will it be?"
Sanni also seemed curious to hear his answer.
"I don't have the exact date yet, but sometime next month. Now listen, Tabitha, I already spoke with Toffy because he has been working on Anita's program for a while. He does the choreography for the dancers of the show. You will have regular rehearsals with him to choreograph your performance."
"Oh, Mies, I am going to need you there."
"Tabitha, please, you don't need me for the rehearsals. You know I have to be in Brazil."
Sanni seemed again curious and asked when he would be in Brazil.
"Next week," Mono answered, "for a couple of days. I have some business there to attend. I am meeting up with Faith."
"Faith, Faith, always Faith," Tabitha complained. "I cannot hear her name anymore!"

Her voice had lost all the excitement, and Sanni acted afraid she might cry.
Mono decided to ignore her last comment and instead turned towards Sanni.
"Come on man," "let's go downstairs to my office, and I will give you Thomas Fuddle's number."
While they walked down the stairs together, he made his second strange request that day.
"Sanni, listen, do me a favor, okay?"
"Sure, man, what can I do?"
"You can spread the word about the video but just don't mention TMF. If anyone asks, just say MTV."
Sanni looked at him with a look of confusion.
"I have my reasons. Trust me."

Sanni behaved glad to have Thomas Fuddle's new number. Sanni thanked Mono several times. Mono kept walking out of the door when a letter on the floor caught his attention. Mono picked the letter up, opened him and began to read its contents. Sanni stopped dead in his tracks as he saw every ounce of color drain from Mono's face.
"Brother, what's wrong?" Sanni asked in a panic. "Are you okay?"
Mono looked up with his mouth partly open, but he didn't say a word. Monos froze in either shock or fear Sanni couldn't quite tell which. Finally, a few words came out of his mouth.

"It's a letter from my lawyers Fischer & Euler in Frankfurt/M. Our project appears to be over."
Sanni's mouth fell open, and his eyes remained full. Mono stayed still, standing in the same spot, rereading the letter shaking his head in disbelief.
Sanni tried to think of something comforting to say. The best he could manage continued, "Holy shit man, there exists something I can do to help you?"
"Thanks, Sanni, but not right now."
Sanni seemed worried but stopped asking.
Mono finally put the letter down on the desk. "Please Sanni," he whispered, "just leave me alone now I need to make some phone calls."
His face remained sheet white, and Sanni had not yet seen him blink his eyes. Sanni didn't want to leave him alone like that, but he did as Mono asked. He walked out of the office turned and said, "Okay, but please, call me if there is anything I can do."
After Sanni had gone, Mono appeared still standing in the middle of the office, frozen in fear. It felt to him as his brain acted bumping against his skull. His eyes stayed magnetically bound to one beige piece of paper on the desk. He switched the stereo automatically on. Peyote - "I Will Fight No More" appeared beating in the office.
"Emerged the moment to admit failure?" It had passed one hour before Mono gained enough composure to return to his apartment. Before he did, he ripped up the letter and burned the shredded bits of paper in an ashtray.
Tabitha saw his pale, sweaty skin and immediately asked what had gone wrong. In her concern, she completely forgets the whole Faith issue.

Tabitha asked him very sweetly, "Where have you been all of the time, Mies?"
"Nowhere, baby," but he seemed not capable of further conversation.
In fact, the only thing he wanted to talk with Faith about it. But of course, he didn't.

Mono opened his eyes early on Saturday morning on the couch. Tabitha acted already in the kitchen, filling two glasses of water for both.
"Morning, babe," he mumbled.
His head did swimming with activity about the news from yesterday.
"Good morning Mies," she smiled. "How are you feeling?"
Tabitha flipped on the coffee machine, and he mumbled that he felt great. The couple' stayed talking until the coffee seemed ready to go.
After the pot had emerged full, Tabitha brought him his doping and sat on the edge of the couch, holding his free hand.
Mono took a sip of the hot coffee, and she asked again if everything remained okay.
"Yes of course. But listen," Mono continued, waking up from the caffeine, "I forgot to mention this yesterday, but I kept thinking about your video clip."
"Thinking what?"

"I believe that we should keep the news to ourselves until we are closer to the broadcast, you know, and at the day we can surprise everyone. How do you feel about it?"
"Well," Tabitha answered hesitantly, "I don't know. Maybe I mean, I guess that's okay. If you think it's a good idea." A smile appeared on Mono's face after she agreed.
U96 - "Das Boot" – Trance Mix played kicking from the speakers in the living room.
"What you think about Thai food for lunch today? I know an awesome restaurant, close to the Red Light district?" Tabitha seemed not to have expected an invitation on a Saturday from Mono. "Are you not working today at all?" Mono acted surprised by her answer. "Do you have plans already?" Tabitha hesitated in a strange way. "I want to meet a friend from school at Hard Rock Cafe. She is in town for the day. I forgot to tell you."
Mono couldn't help it, but the scene Tabitha jumped into a car in front of his house a while ago emerged in his mind.

It appeared to be already Tuesday, and Mono still had not completely recovered. He continued to rack his brain, searching for some solution to the impossible dilemma. No obvious answer pops up in his mind. He decided to call his mother in Germany. Mono did not tell her about the bad events in his life right now. His mother felt like moms feel, and she kept asking, "Junge what's wrong?" he vehemently denied that anything wrong occurred. His mother already had enough trouble with his sick father, and he did not want to bother her with his problems. Rather, he would wait until he is in Germany and tells them the whole wild story in person. Only hearing her voice helped him to get back on track.

Mono remembered that he still needed a ride to the airport.

He mechanically dialed Nakka D's number and asked for a lift to the airport the next morning. He explained to Nakka D that he departure at three in the morning and Nakka D promised to pick him up at his house in time.

Mono stood waiting on the sidewalk at 1:30 in the morning. The street appeared completely dark until the headlights from Nakka D's car came around the corner. The car stopped, the trunk popped open, and he threw in two big suitcases. He slammed the hood shut and walked around to the open door, where he slid into the passenger seat.

The first words out of Nakka D's mouth seemed an apology.

"Sorry, man," he shrugged, "I'm kind of late. But there are almost no cars on the road at this hour so we should make it to the airport quickly."

He stared straight ahead and said numbly, "I guess so."

Nakka D expected a stronger reaction, and he asked him if everything remained okay. Normally he never let tardiness go unnoticed, even with his friends.

But Nakka D got no response to his first question; he tried another one.

"Where is Tabitha?" he asked. "Isn't she coming with us?"

"No," he said, still staring ahead, "she just went to bed."

Mono is still acting funny, Nakka D thought to himself. Still tired and stoned from the evening's partying, Nakka D decided to let it pass.

They drove straight through the city center, where everything stayed eerily quiet. The silence became uncomfortable; Mono began up a conversation.

"I've meant to tell you, man, I listened to DJ Ruff's tape together with some friends of mine.

No, wait!" he suddenly shouted and pointed out the window.

"Wait," he said again, "it's better if you take the next right here. There is construction a block away."

Nakka D nodded and took a sharp right.

"Anyway," he went on, "we listened to the tape a few times, and we all agree that your guy has potential. So we are going to help him out. "Tribe Movement," friends of ours, will produce an "Ibiza Reunion" show in Amsterdam soon. You can tell your cousin that he will be the opening DJ for the night."
Nakka D took his attention from the road and slapped him hi-five.
"Oh man," Nakka D cried, "that is so great. DJ Ruff will be very fucking happy for sure."
Mono not yet finished, though. He still had to ask Nakka D for one thing.
"Look, Nakka D, can you please ask your cousin not to mention the show to anyone until I am back from Brazil? I know it sounds strange, but I have my reasons. What do you think?"
Nakka D didn't need any time to think. His excitement had not diminished one bit.
"It still sounds great to me Thanks, man!"
"You are always welcome Nakka D and please say hi to DJ Ruff for me."
Mono made it to the airport in plenty of time.

VII

Everything Gonna Be All Right

Faith's plane continued scheduled to arrive two hours later from Miami. Mono acted surprised when Faith tapped him on the shoulder as he waited on line for "Aduana," or Brazilian customs.
"Wow, what are you doing here?"
Mono had an enormous grin on his face and dropped his bags to give her a hug.
She felt a strange intensity almost electricity in the hug.
"Hey! I thought I might run into you here. Surprise! My plane didn't leave Miami until early this morning, and I continued sitting waiting in the airport for hours. I am so glad to be away from that damn plane. Thank god for the red wine."
"Tell me about it. I had a long layover at Charles de Gaulle; I switched planes.

Both followed one another through the customs inspection and out into the greeter's lobby. Thomas, the German Doctor, arrived already waiting there, waving his arms in their direction.

"Look, there's Thomas. Exactly on time like always if only all Brazilians acted as punctual."

They shared a laugh as they walked over to Thomas. Both had spent enough time in the country to know that punctuality meant not to be a Brazilian trait. Thomas, however, was born in Germany and had never adapted to the Brazilian schedule.

"My friend Thomas thanks so much for picking us up here," Mono said.

"Yes, Thomas," "thanks happily I am the one who had the delayed flight."

"You guys are welcome; it took about fifty minutes to get here. We should get back in even less time. Let's go; my car is parked right out front."

Both followed Thomas's lead and headed outside into the sticky summer night.

"So tell me, what has been going on in Amsterdam these past few weeks? You have been impossible to get in touch with."

"Tell me about it," she added with a wink. "I always had to call at least five times before I could find him." Mono smiled and began to recount the latest weeks in Amsterdam.

"I'm sorry for being difficult to contact for you guys. The beginning of the year has been crazy. Things got interesting. Apparently, someone made an attempt to sabotage Tabitha's performance on TV. Can you believe that?

Both acted shocked, especially Thomas, who despised any underhanded business.

"You need to watch out for Tabitha," he said.

Mono switched over to a thoughtful face.

They appeared all left to deep thoughts for the rest of the ride. As per Thomas's prediction, they arrived cruising down Avenida Paulista forty-five minutes later.

"There, Thomas," Mono pointed, "turn to Rua Augusta and make the first left, please. We are right at the spot."

Thomas pulled his minivan up the ramp in front of the Santos Flat Service. The doorman ran outside and greeted Mono with a hearty "Tudo bom?" It had been a while since he last stayed there, but all the workers at the apartment service loved him. "I hope you like this place," he said to Faith. "The rooms are beautiful, and the service here is excellent and all affordable."

Mono went on to Thomas. "Thank you again for the ride. We will meet you at your office at Paradiso at nine tomorrow morning, greetings to Adriana."

"Excellent, alright, guys, I will call you in a little time. Have a beautiful day!"

She continued peering into her apartment, "As always, you pick the most beautiful places."

"Thanks for the vote of confidence. You have some pretty classy taste yourself."

"Well, maybe. Now listen," Faith said thoughtfully, "I can see in your face that there is more bothering you that you seemed willing to mention in front of Thomas."

"You know me well."

"Yes, and now I want to know what's going on. How about this? Let's both take quick showers and leave the unpacking for later. We can eat some sushi somewhere in Jardins and talk about things over a bottle of sake."

Realizing her offer sounded more personal than she had intended, "Anyway, we should have a chance to discuss business before tomorrow's meeting."

He didn't need any convincing. He could already taste the hot miso soup. He picked up his bags and walked to his apartment at the end of the hall.

"Alright, I will be knocking on your door in thirty minutes. And this time, the sushi is on me!"

They walked leisurely along Rua Haddock Lobo, in the heart of Jardins, Sao Paulo's vibrant neighborhood. Faith kept tripping on loose stones in the sidewalk' because she could not take her eyes off all the buildings. She acted staring up at the massive penthouses and helipads on every other roof.

"Wow," she gushed, "I have never seen this side of the city before. I didn't think Brazil could be classy. These apartment buildings are beautiful. And look at all the nice clothing stores. I am going to be in trouble tomorrow afternoon."
She seemed addicted to window shopping.
"I am glad you like it. I guessed you would. So, where should we get this sushi you promised?"
She pointed diagonally across the street. Mono had no idea what she appeared looking at and crossed the road to get a closer look.
"How do you do it? You can see these things from a mile away!"
She always seemed overly aware of her surroundings. Mono swore that she needed about one day in a new city to become as familiar with the area as a resident. It appeared to be a trait that always came in handy during all travels.
"You know me," she said smugly. "Now come on, I'm starving!"

They ordered a sushi combination for two and bowls of miso soup to start. And, of course, they asked for a flask of hot sake. Faith did the ordering, as she appeared to be the one who could speak the language fluently.

They waited until the first shot of sake emerged warm in their bellies to start the conversation. "Why didn't you tell me that there existed a problem with Tabitha's TV performance, you had the chance in L.A.?"
"It happened to be not important anymore at this point. We switched topics this day so often. I forgot about it that weekend."
"It occurred important enough to tell Thomas about it a few weeks later; sometimes I don't understand you."
Mono apologized and jumped right into the heart of the serious business problem.
Faith listened intensely. "Did you talk to your parents about it?" "No, but we spoke for a half of an hour yesterday. My mom can feel when I am in trouble.
"Okay," she said hesitantly, "How's your dad?"
"Not bad, thanks for asking." Faith took a few quiet minutes to absorb the news and sip the steaming miso soup. "I guess it means we need to work with an alternative plan?"
"I love your unemotional perspective. Yes, we do."
Just at this moment, the sushi arrived, and the colorful boat instantly captured their full attention. They both stabbed the chopsticks at the same volcano roll. Faith began talking again.
"The uncertainties and most importantly work adding up now. We should maybe cancel the whole project?"
Mono felt uncomfortable at this moment.
"Quitting isn't an option at all. I have a plan."
"That sounds promising to me, give me the big picture please."

Faith kept thinking about it, finishing her Sushi at the time. "I am with you, but I can't help it. It's imperative to clone "our plant" later on."

At 8:oo the following morning, Faith and Mono met for breakfast in the dining room. Fresh Ham, delicious Minas cheese, eggs, papaya, and strong, black coffee - the typical Brazilian start to the day happened to be.
The partners' walked together all the way down Avenida Paulista with a refreshing energizing morning sun right in their smiling faces as an early day present. The producers' enjoyed a good walk always, particularly before a business meeting. At 8:55 am both arrived at Thomas's office building. Thomas appeared upstairs waiting at the MBB rooms. "Morning, Thomas," both said in unison. The group, all shook hands and sat down at the desk in the corner. The smell of frying dough wafted through the open window, accompanied by the ever-present construction noise from Paulista. Since the parties had already caught with each other up the evening before on the phone, it emerged nothing to discuss except DJ Peran's album project. Thomas took control of the meeting; both stayed in his territory now.

"We agreed on the details of our contract, but let me go over it once more. My record label will release the album. Your production company will deliver the master CD, a marketing campaign and the artwork for the entire project, ready to go. We do the physical distribution and all advertising in Brazil. The wholesale price will be $2.50 per unit. Worldwide distribution goes to your company in California after a pre-order of 2000 units is confirmed."

"It sounds perfect for our side, Thomas."

Faith jumped in.

"Our lawyer has all the details we already discussed. Is there anything you would like to add before I have it written up?" Both parties appeared to be happy with the achieved so far.

"Alright," Mono reached into his briefcase to pull out documents. He handed the papers to Thomas who scrutinized every word.

"This is the wish DJ list I mentioned. The list is still open of course."

Thomas continued to analyze the list. Still flipping through the list, Thomas sounded nervous. "All of the DJs on your list are almost unknown in Brazil. The electronic dance music market, it's like a newly discovered species right now, and progressive trance isn't even part of the evolution yet. Do you realize how difficult it will be to market the album in Sao Paulo alone?

"Yes," Faith assured him, "we understand this. That is the reason we want to give the project to you. We have total confidence that we can do a great thing together."

"Let's help to get these DJs along the music popular in Brazil. The Internet will contribute to spread the message. Music is traveling faster than ever before in the history of humankind. Five continents are just five computers now. These DJs and producers' are top and hot in their home territories. The movement is growing. It will be like this everywhere." Mono explained with a calm voice.

Thomas's forehead still wrinkled in worry, and he kept looking down at the list. The partners, both not sure of a good ending at this moment just stirred in Thomas direction.
Thomas smiled and asked Mono. "How much money do you have in your pocket right now?"
Mono wondered but checked his pockets. "I have 1400 Reais in cash on me."
"This is very too much money to walk around with in Sao Paulo. Even in the day time, I will keep it with me as an advance payment. Is it cool with you guys?"
Mono and Faith smiling agreed.
Thomas continued.
"Okay, let MBB join the movement. I will confirm with DJ Peran. But, instead of him recording in Sao Paulo, why don't we save the money and have him recorded at his studio in the Netherlands? You guys are putting in all the money, so every bit helps. Plus, Mono could be in Amsterdam to make sure everything goes smoothly in the studio."

"Let see where we are after all requirements of our project emerge established, but this seems an option," Mono contributed.
All seemed satisfied and nodded in agreement. Before the partners had a chance to add another thought, however, Thomas jumped in again.
"I need a promo record as soon as possible I want something to present to my partners in Sao Paulo."
Mono opened his briefcase and took two tape boxes and an envelope out. "Take these trance music demos, recently recorded in Amsterdam - The Funky Fakirs. The song list is enclosed." "I know you would arrive in Sao Paulo prepared, thank you. Have you guys a time frame regarding the release date?" Mono watched in the direction of Faith. "What will be the name of the album?" Thomas asked.
This time, she fielded the questions.
"Well, first of all, we want to release the album when the time is right. Down the road, it's a very complex project. In nine months we present a modified schedule to MBB. Regarding the name, we go with a working title for now. Is that okay with you? What do you think?"
"Apparently we just started a German, Dutch, Brazilian and American trance music project. I agree on your relaxed approach." Thomas pointed out.
"Moving on," Thomas said, "so what are your plans for Brazil?"
"We will be working in Rio for the next few days. "We will come back to Sao Paulo before we leave the country. That way we can have another meeting with the three of us."

"Why don't you send me an email when you are back? Adriana, and I will meet you two for dinner? We have an excellent new Japanese restaurant just at the end of Avenida Paulista."
Both looked at each other and shared a smile. Neither of the couple' could object to another sushi feast.
The meeting appeared over, and all stayed satisfied with the results.
"I hope you guys have a nice time in Rio," Thomas wished as a good buy.

Both spent the evening at a party at Sao Paulo's great Love e-club.
"The LGS crowd loves its hard techno," Faith commented.
The next morning they picked up the rental car and headed out to the Dutra highway. The sign said 450 kilometers to Rio de Janeiro. For the first hour, they sat in the steamy traffic, alongside thousands of Paulistas escaping the city for the refuge of the beach. Finally, they reached the countryside and Faith stared out the window at the passing coconut stands and banana plants.
"Brazilian cows are the ugliest in the world."
"I know Indian cows; they look strange to everyone. Check out that sign over there; the place has corn-flavored ice cream. I bet you would love it. Maybe we will stop on the way back."
"That would be the best."

Three hours later the partners' appeared driving through the suburbs of Rio and soon arrived on Avenida Brasil, surrounded by buses spitting out the gray smoke that clouded the air.
"Just follow the signs for Zona Sul," she directed. "And look for the sign that points to Copacabana." Suddenly Mono's cellular phone began to ring.
"Hello?"
"It's Olga here."
The connection stayed terrible.
"How is Brazil?"
"Great," Mono shouted, "but go ahead and tell me what's going on. Your call is expensive."
"Well," Olga said nervously, "I already sent you an email. Did you get it?"
"I got your email."
Faith lowered the music from the radio.
"Listen, I know these are your matters, but I needed to tell you. I mean, after I saw Tabitha kissing some guy at the Hard Rock Cafe, I thought for sure you would want to know."
"Olga is turning into Sherlock Holmes."
"I am sorry," she apologized, but I thought you should know it's a business matter."
"I appreciate your loyalty," "but there is something you should be aware. Tabitha and I had ended our relationship before I left for Brazil." Mono felt how the news exploded at the office in Amsterdam. He went on. "Don't worry; we will continue with our professional relationship as it is. Olga, we can talk about it later. I will let you go now, thank you for your call I appreciate it." Mono hung up the phone and just said, "Jesus!"

"You acted lying!"
"Yes, on all issues."
"I have a clue about it but tell me why?"
Mono appeared shocked searching for the right words. He couldn't find an explication directly.
"I trust my instincts, and they acted telling it to me. Think about it; it's better this way it will stop rumors before some begin flying around in Amsterdam. We don't want drama."
Faith agreed with his views, but she seemed worried. "All angles change fast it appears. What about your big plan of the planting? Tabitha emerged imperative for your plan."
They drove the rest of the way to Wuff's place in Copacabana in silence just listening to Pagode from the radio.

Mono broke the silence after both arrived at Wuff's home. He switched to a beautiful theme. "I have been in love with Rio since the very first time I came here."
"Yeah," "you are right. Just look at this view. It is so amazing to see the landscape, right?"
Soon they seemed both staring dreamily off the apartment balcony, enjoying a panoramic view of sunny Copacabana. To the left they could see the cable cars ascending Pao de Acucar and behind them stood the famous Cristo statue, embracing the entire city.
Faith asked when Wuff would be coming home.

"Six o'clock. So we have just enough time to go for a walk to Ipanema and back."
She agreed wholeheartedly, and both headed out the door."

"Wow, Wuff, you are such an amazing cook," Faith declared in between giant bites of chicken curry. "It makes me so sad that we will have to leave again on Monday evening."
Wuffi the German clubber gave her a giant hug, and Faith, completely enveloped by his big sweaty body.
"I am sure you will be back in Rio soon enough."
Faith's face appeared to be full of skepticism.
"I am not so sure about that, Wuffi," she said sadly.
"I have so much work to do in Miami. The only chance I have of coming back is if we produce the show here. I would for sure come down again, at least for a few days. I guess we will know when Mono gets back from the meeting," Actually she realized, "Mono should already be here by now."
"Yeah, well, you know him," Wuffi said in his gruff, friendly voice. "He knows people in this city, and it has been a while since he occurred last in town. Maybe he ran into somebody on the way back from his appointment. I am sure he will be here soon."
Faith had a question for Wuffi.
"I have been wondering," she said curiously "how long have you guys known each other?"
"Oh, Faith, since the end 80s," Wuffi reminisced.
"Mono become a regular at Marilyn, my 24/7 club in Lampertheim. Our friendship goes back to the trance after party roots."

Sirena - "Spring of Life" continued grooving from the sound system in the living room.
"Yeah, that I can feel since I know you guys."
Right then, the door opened, and Mono came in.
"What can you see, Faith?" Mono asked.
Both acted laughing at his question.
Mono said seriously, "Come on, guys, we have to talk I just don't know if we should produce this show here."
"Why? What is the offer?"
"Well, money-wise, it occurred exciting. But the main point is that we would have only until the end of March to produce the entire event. We would need a co - producer in Rio to take care of everything. We would have to supervise the whole production via telephone and email. We are only a plan b option to them anyway. They had a producer for six months on the project. He canceled the contract recently. The agency acted searching for a replacement now."
Neither of them had an answer.
"Well, what appears to your mind?" Faith asked.
"I don't know do you have any ideas here?
"Maybe Fabio Flyer could help us out."
Mono not convinced by her suggestion. "Fabio is a very great guy but too inexperienced. Who want to bring Sven Väth to Rio de Janeiro Wuff?"
"Rick Rainer."
"That's the guy. With this guy, I would like to work one day."
Mono announced, "Anyway there is no way for us to handle the job especially with all of these problems going on in Amsterdam. You guys have any other opinions regarding our matter?"

"Yes, you are right I agree."
Wuff recognized the sad look they exchanged and appeared confused.
"What's going on, guys? Did I miss something?"
Mono nodded and began to explain the situation, starting from the day he received that letter in Amsterdam and finishing with Olga's call from a day before. Wuff's eyes bulged, but he said nothing so that Mono could finish his story.
"And that is not all," Mono continued. "It seemed somebody is trying to sabotage Tabitha's carrier in Amsterdam."
Wuff shook his head. "How did you find out about it?"
"Well, like news travels in the entertainment world. Do you remember Silke the German model and her habit to get picked up by celebrities?"
"Sure I do our Barbie. I miss her."
"Yeah, well Silke picked up a guy at the "Energy Hours" party. The man appeared high on Coke and told her the wild sabotage story but didn't disclose the source. Silke called me the next evening and told me all about it."
"What did you do about it?"
"I had party with Silke. It appeared not much I could do but believing in "our force." Of course, I am still worried. I have never imagined anything like it could happen. I am very blue-eyed sometimes. I am blonde what can I do?"
"Orchestrated by whom?"
"I have an exquisite guess but no proof."
"You need to be watching your back, my friend. That's not right."

Mono hugged Wuff.
"I keep him telling that," Faith added and acted a bit jealous. Mono felt uncomfortable and switched the topic. "By the way, Wuff your friend Rinus van Kooten, the Dutch geek, installed his new supercomputer in our office. He and Eric Nouhan are sending warm greetings to you."
Wuff appeared smiling hearing the news.

First thing on Monday morning Faith called to Gene's office in Miami.
"Good morning Gene."
"Oh. I just got into the office. You have the right timing."
"Maybe, but I also know you stick to a very precise schedule. I remained entirely sure that I would find you at precisely 8:30, walking in from breakfast."
"You got me there," Gene laughed. "So what can I do for you Faith? How ended up your meeting in Sao Paulo?"
"Actually," "that is why I am calling. We are ready to go ahead with the contract, exactly as we already discussed."
"Alright guys, I can have my secretary prepare the papers for tomorrow evening."

Faith seemed satisfied, knowing that the contract would probably be ready even earlier. While Gene acted as the company's general counsel, he happened to be a key player in business development as well. In other words, Gene would raise the money the project needs. She moved on to her second reason for calling. "There are more topics. Our plans have changed drastically since we last spoke. We need more financial support for our project and, most importantly, we need it as soon as possible."
Faith explained to Gene the happenings besieging the business in Europa.
Gene needed some time to consider the possibilities. He responded with some question regarding the issues.
"Wow," Gene mused, "it does change everything. And, unfortunately, I do not have a quick solution to offer you. However, there is one thing that I know for sure we are going to have to do. We need to open a new company, and I suggest we incorporate in the state of Florida."
"Did I hear you correctly, Gene?" "Are you saying we need to start over?"
Faith voice got louder with every word, and by the time she ended the conversation, she appeared nearly whining in frustration. Nodding her head saying, "I don't have the power to resolve it it's very over my head."

Mono walked out of his bedroom and saw the frustrated look on her face.

"Wow, it finished a tough conversation for you. Shock me more what did Gene have to say?"

"Look," she sighed, "we only have a little bit more time to spend. Why don't we first go for a walk on the beach? That way we can discuss everything and still enjoy our last moments in Rio." As always, she had already planned everything in her head. Mono followed her lead, and they both slid into the matching Havaianas sandals before leaving the apartment. They flip-flopped down the street, and when they arrived at the beach, they turned in the direction of Ipanema. They walked and tossed ideas back and forth. Mono felt it seemed enough to talk about the project and pushed a freshly cut coconut under her nose. Faith drank almost half the coconut in one sip and let the cold liquid run through her body. Mono liked her happy face.

"Wow, look how far we are already," "we are at the park Garota de Ipanema."

"How wonderful continues it." Faith said.

They crossed the park and went straight to the beach. The beach packed with surfers and muscle men doing pull-ups on rusty bars. Mono took her hand and led her out onto the giant rock that separated Rio's most famous beaches. They hiked together until they reached the edge closest to the water and sat down on the rocks.

"Another fantastic view in the Cidade Maravilhosa," he said dreamily.

"You know what they say about this rock, right?"

"No, but please tell me."

"Well," he answered mysteriously, "If you look at the water and make a wish on your first time at this place, it will come real."
She smiled at him and looked out at the water, concentrating hard on her dream.
"Just don't tell me your wish," he teased.
By then, she acted no longer staring at the water. Instead, she appeared staring into Mono's shiny blue eyes.
Mono stirred back wordlessly, and his eyes sparkled with intensity.
The kiss seemed pure electricity. The waves crashed loudly against the rocks. Faith and Mono are in love. Neither of them caught any glimpse of the vibrant green landscape during the drive back to Sao Paulo. Both acted deep into a conversation about the power that made paths cross at "Wuff's Rotary" club in Rio de Janeiro less than a year ago. The day they both met for the first time.
Arriving at the apartment building, both rushed up to his apartment on the fifth floor. Faith arms embraced his body as he quickly opened the door. Dropping the luggage right where both stood, they began ripping the clothes off each other's bodies. He acted so nervously and excited that he struggled to put the condom on his dick. After only minutes of fervid fucking, they both came in an explosion of screams and spasms. The sex occurred intense but gentle, and they lay together for the next hour, speechless and breathless

The next morning Faith fixed a lovely breakfast of eggs, fruit, and toast and a very special coffee for him. Mono sang his special "La La" song from the bed, and she acted laughing in the kitchen.

But the paradise could not last forever. The lovers' had to come back to reality and prepare for the crucial meeting with Thomas.

"We need to keep everything honest with Thomas."

"Of course there is no other way to deal with it."

The couple' walked down Avenida Paulista once more, but this time walking hand in hand. Neither said a word the whole trip. Both appeared too nervous.

The spectacular events of the previous day gave Faith a new confidence. She could feel his strength inside her, and she acted as the controlling presence in the meeting.

Thomas hung on to Faith's every word, without a single interruption.

"Okay, you guys," Thomas said firmly, "I will give your new company the worldwide distribution, sub-publishing and digital rights for my records. You will be the only ones who can market my records anywhere except in Brazil."

Thomas, always the businessman, continued to lay out the details.

"I will need to know all of your marketing plans so I can work it into my schedule."

"Sure," in Mono's first comment on the meeting. "I will email you all the information you need as soon as we have a filing date for the new company and all of the requirements established."

"You can count on getting all the information in a month," she added.
Walking out of Thomas's office building, Mono and Faith felt confident that the project made an excellent choice for a business partner. The lovers' took a detour from Avenida Paulista and wandered for an hour through Jardins, planning all next steps in the game. It appeared to be, in the scheme of things, just a game.
The farewell the next morning emerged tearfully. At the airport, the couple' shared a long passionate kiss. Both hoped it developed as the beginning of something incredible.

VIII

Hanky–Panky

Back in Amsterdam, Mono inquisitive called Tabitha to schedule a business meeting. Groove Solution - "Magic Melody" kept going from the stereo in the room. She acted friendly with her greeting, but her response appeared chilly.

"I am sorry," Tabitha explained, "but I cannot meet today. I have a manager, from now on you will have to speak with my manager about any professional matters first."

She sounded ridiculous, but he seemed too tired to laugh or fight. "Okay Tabitha," he sighed, exasperated. "Please tell me with whom I should speak to schedule a meeting with you."

There had emerged an awkward silence before she answered the question.

"Mies, my manager is my mother."

"Tabitha. Can you please be so kind as to ask her to set up a meeting for us as soon as possible? She can choose the day."

They both had to laugh at that weird situation.

"Love you, Tabitha," he thought after hanging up the phone.

Faith spent her entire first day back in Miami at Gene's law office in North Miami Beach. Faith and Gene sat at the conference table eating turkey subs from Quizno's and discussing the game plan.

"Okay, I have completed the incorporation papers and my secretary will fax them to the Department of Corporations in Tallahassee. As soon as they receive the documents, we will have a case number. You can go ahead and call the IRS toll free number. In about ten minutes you will have a federal tax identification number for the new company. Pretty quick, huh?"

"Wow, I never realized how easy this could be. Although nothing is ever as easy as it seems first." Gene had been practicing law for thirty years and, with his Harvard law degree, he always managed to do things quickly and efficiently. It only looked dull when he finished.

"Now," she continued, "we will need to get a new bank account in Florida, but I will have to wait until we have the tax number. I already checked out the Bank of America website. We can fill out the entire application online once we have that number. Pretty quick, huh?" she teased.

Gene laughed and opened his mouth to make a smart comment when her cell phone rang in her purse.

The screen said only "incoming call" she answered like it seemed a telemarketer.

"Yeah?"

"Happy Valentine's Day for you honey."

"Hey!" she said in surprise, "I'm sorry, I didn't know it could be you. Thank you so much for thinking of me."

She excused herself from the conference room and went out to the hall for a bit of privacy.

"Honey," he whispered, "I miss you very much. I can barely concentrate on my work."

"Oh, I know what you mean. I miss you like hell."

"Yeah, I know. So tell me, what are you up to in Miami?"

"I am actually at Gene's office right now. We happened to be eating some lunch since we just finished all the paperwork. By the same time next week, we should have everything we need to get the Florida Corporation off the ground."

"One thing more," she continued. "The office in Los Angeles will be closed by the end of the month. We only will keep the address, all is good."

"You are the most amazing woman I have ever met."

She giggled but caught his trick.

"You stole that line from the Titanic movie. But I know you mean every word."

Just after she hung up the cell phone, she remembered to ask about his first meeting with Tabitha; she made her mind up not to call back and went back into the conference room.

Mono truly appreciated Amsterdam's watery splendor. However, sometimes even the breathtaking scenery failed to overcome the city's dreary weather. Dull gray clouds obscured the blue sky, but life within the record label's office remained brimming with its usual activity. Olga's ear appeared glued to the phone while he enticed Jo with tales of Brazil and its fabulous landscapes and sexy girls. The sound of Third Bass continued beating in the background. Mono's descriptions were detailed and colorful. He kept a special place in his heart for Brazil and Jo acted clearly impressed.

"I need to visit this country," Jo gushed.

"Well, you'd better hurry up and go," he answered, "because the girls are getting restless!"

They both erupted into laughter, drawing Olga's attention away from the telephone. She quickly ended her conversation and turned to inquire what could be so funny.

"Guy talk," Mono teased.

"Oh, please," she snorted, "you're like two little boys." The laughter stopped, but both looked only slightly apologetic.

"Anyway," Olga continued, "that was Tabitha's mother on the phone just now. She is coming to the office tomorrow she will bring her lawyer. Both will be here at 8 PM. It will be a late appointment."

And, without giving them any time to respond, Olga looked straight at him and said, "Don't even say it! She swears that after tomorrow morning she is booked solid for the next days."

Mono got up from his chair, stood at attention, and saluted sharply.

"I have nothing to say, Olga."
He turned to Jo with a smirk and said, "Maybe we should bring a razor to the office tomorrow. With a tongue that sharp, she might need a new one."
Both Jo and Olga groaned.
Jo scolded, "Your German jokes are just not funny at all. Everyone knows that this weird German humor doesn't translate into any other language!"
Mono unsuccessfully racked his brain for a sharp retort until rescued by his buzzing telephone.
Iris, the German friend, appeared on the other end of the line.

Peter and Hartmut appeared huddled together in Hartmut's private office, located just off Amsterdam's Rozengracht, smack in the center of the city.
Peter took charge of the discussion, speaking decisively but quietly.
"So tell me, Hartmut," he asked proudly, "what did you think of my using a person as a candy for Tabitha?"
Hartmut smiled but answered only after a bit of thought.
"A hint from your friend Juup made that happen, Peter? You guys have certainly put together one great couple. Still, Tabitha will do all of her shows in the coming twelve months."
"No way," Peter answered.

"Well, I'm still not sure about your big plan," Hartmut went on hesitantly. "I can see the dynamics of our situation just as well as you."
Hartmut's voice raised a notch as he continued, "But now, Peter, are you seriously telling me that we need to convince Eric to sign with Mono? Can I ask what the hell is going on in your head here?"
Peter stared back patiently, leaving Hartmut to continue with his rant.
"I just don't understand you, Peter."
Finally, Peter jumped in to calm down his friend.
Peter appeared grinning from ear to ear. "Just think about it, I would control his label!"
"Are you kidding? That is not easy. I know Mono since few years!"
"Nothing is easy in this business, Hartmut, I know that." Peter continued.
"And actually," "I honestly do like the name of this guy's album project. "Magic Inspiration" it's cool."
"Peter, your sarcasm is not becoming. I just hope you can maintain control of this whole crazy situation and that nobody else gets hurt along the way."
Peter ignored the skepticism; he stood up and shook Hartmut's hand with a smile.
"I will see myself out of the office, my friend."

It appeared to be 7 PM, and Mono occurred sitting alone in his room, waiting for Tabitha's mother and her lawyer.

Having made some progress, Mono appeared satisfied with the work of the team. It emerged no wonder that he happened to be in an excellent mood. With an hour's time before the scheduled appointment, he continued to study the contract for the Eric Nouhan album. The terms remained ok as far as Mono could tell. However, something else happened bothering him. Mono knows that this album could be a big energy boost for the project in the Netherlands. On the other hand, RW Records could lose a lot of precious time with the album. Mono reviewed his options from all possible angles several times. Lastly, he faxed the signed contract back to Eric Nouhan.

The clock had just turned 7.30 PM when he heard the jingle of his doorbell. Knowing it seemed a little too early for Tabitha's mother; he looked suspiciously at the monitor from his front door surveillance camera. Waiting on the steps appeared his friend Milton, who was just about the last person he expected to see at that hour. Mono walked to the front door and found Milton greeting him with a broad, friendly smile.

"Sorry to bother you at this hour," "but I did passing by and saw the light on in your office."

"No problem, brother," he beckoned his friend into the vestibule. "Come on in and have a seat."

They walked together into the only lit room within the office. Mono returned to his recliner and Milton; the friendly Dutch flopped down in the chair in front of the desk.

"So tell me, what's going on these days, how is your lovely girlfriend Milton? What's new in the city?

"She is busy but great. Nothing new, the same shit is always going on here."
Milton opened his bag and pulled out some rolling papers to make a joint but Mono promptly interrupted his activity.
"Sorry, brother, I have a lawyer coming by in a little while, we will have to postpone the smoking session until after the meeting."
"Oh, sorry," Milton said sheepishly, "I will let you to your work. I didn't mean to disturb you."
Mono smiled, and Milton seemed a little more relaxed.
"No big deal," he assured him. "I may need a witness tonight you have a job now, stick around."

At that, Mono heard the front door jingle again. This time he didn't bother to check the monitor, as he remained rather confident of his visitors' identities. He sauntered out of the office and opened the front door without hesitation. His mouth dropped in surprise as he saw that it appeared not Tabitha's mother greeting him with her usual warm smile. Three huge guys stood in the doorway, the massive bodies obscuring the light from the overhead fixture. Before he could recover from his surprise and think of something to say, the guy in the middle shoved him hard in the chest and after half-carried him back into the office.

Behind him, he heard Milton scream, "What the hell do you guys want?"

The group did wearing bulletproof vests as a striking accessory to the scary appearance.

The thugs pushed Mono into his seat behind the desk. Mono tried to protest, but it seemed useless.

"Shut up," the biggest thug yelled, "or be prepared to meet your maker."

"What bad movie is that from?" Mono mused to himself.

Mono noted that their broken English appeared characterized by a thick Eastern European accent.

"Listen, you mother fucker," one guy growled, "for you, there is no more breathing space in this city. You will leave in the next 48 hours, or you will be history. Do you get it?" To make the point more clear the smallest man of these three kicked one of the office chairs as it was a football. The furniture crashed into the wall and took a print from a Kandinsky painting down, breaking it into pieces. Neither he nor Milton remembered who acted first to manage a meek response.

"OK."

Only minutes later, the two stayed once again alone in the office, shocked and speechless, but unharmed. Mono still shaking regained his composure and looked over to Milton who seemed already anxiously rolling a large joint.

Milton commented dryly, "Maybe you should change the lawyers you do business with?"

Both erupted in loud nervous laughter.

"Milton, I am glad as hell you stayed here. These guys would have seriously fucked me up otherwise."

They smoked the entire joint in silence, each lost in deep thoughts.

On his way out, Milton repeated, "Don't forget, I am always around whenever you need me." Mono gave Milton a big Hug. "Give greetings to your family. Don't talk with anyone about it ok brother?" Milton assured him of it and left.

As the door closed loudly, Mono saw that he had a voice message on his phone. After he had listened to the message, he dialed 911.

"This is unbelievably horrible!" Faith wailed. "What did the police say to you? Please, tell me everything! I don't understand!"

She appeared out of her mind, and his attempts to calm her down seemed so far unsuccessful.

"Please honey, relax. The policemen are watching my house, and they will continue to take care for me until they can figure out who emerged responsible for the attack."

"And you trust them?"

"Listen," Mono explained. "When I first got to the police station, they didn't care about my wild mafia thug story, and I felt lost. But after I played a recording of the guy threatening my life on my phone's voice mail, they couldn't help but be with me. You should hear this guy's voice and the shit he said." Immediately he regretted his last comment.

"Anyway," he went on, "my point is that the police are at the story and I am sure, the cops are making the job one-hundred percent."
Faith acted entirely unconvinced.
"Please, you have to get the hell out of that city!"
"It's not Amsterdam! I love this city." Mono went on.
"That is impossible right now. What am I supposed to do, drop everything and leave? Look, I promise you I will be very careful and watch out for myself."
"Do you think Tabitha has anything to do with it?"
"Tabitha doesn't have any motive," "I don't think she could have had anything to do with it."
"Are you blind?"
"No," he protested with his voice rising, "I am not blind. I am sure Tabitha isn't involved in it. Money, jealousy, envy, hatred, desire who knows a lot could be a motive in either case powerful hidden forces are at work. Without any evidence, we can't blame anybody at this point."
She sighed deeply, overcome by emotion and fear. Her heart worked in pain as she thought about her love so far away and in so much danger.
He hadn't finished ruminate over the situation.
"Okay, you are right that I had an appointment with Tabitha's mother, who never showed up. I don't know anymore. The key is for the police to find all of the hard facts in the case. All I can do is going on with my life here. Tomorrow morning I am supposed to be in the studio with Tabitha."
She could see through his facade. She knew he occurred just as scared as she acted.
"Please, don't act so tough."

"Honey, I promise you, I take this severe, will rethink everything in the coming days, and I will come up with a solution. Good, honey? What do you think?" He asked hopefully.

As he had hoped, his words had a relaxing effect, and she spoke for the first time with some confidence about the situation.

"I will never understand how you can handle this shit so easy. However, I don't believe that Tabitha will show up at the studio tomorrow morning."

"How could she?" Mono responded, "She doesn't even know about the appointment. I will call her mother as soon as we get off the phone. And I will not say a word about the evening. You can be sure that neither will she."

"Okay," she conceded, "just please send me an email later on so that I know that everything is okay with you."

He promised to do it, but he acted not ready to end the conversation just yet.

"I have one last wish, honey," he murmured.

"What!" she yelped after hearing his request? "How can you think for a second about phone sex? You must be crazy. I am sorry, but I am just not in the mood for that right now."

"Okay, fine honey, I love you, and we will talk tomorrow. "Faith hung up the phone and stared down at the gray shag carpet, deep in anxious thought.

"God," she murmured, "we need some new carpet!"

Even her jokes couldn't lighten her mood that late afternoon. But even with her thoughts a thousand miles away, she acted determinedly to get back to work.
She decided to inform Gene about the new obstacles and went straight to his room. Gene appeared sitting behind his desk and listened carefully to Faith's strange story.
Their Florida Corporation began fully active, and Faith seemed comfortable in the new Miami office, but she had yet to get the website up according to the big plan. Unfortunately, she remained in over her head with this computer stuff.
She clicked open her Outlook mailbox and sighed as all the new emails popped up. There appeared emails from programmers around the world, each of them written in a language she would never understand. She first read the latest mail from the new website designer and checked on the progress of the site. Again, the words stayed blurry within the bright purple and yellow design. She churned out a quick mail to Michelle Echevarria the designer in New York City and hit the send button, but not before sending a carbon copy to him in Amsterdam.

Faith's eyes acted on fire in front of the computer monitor, and her mind appeared a blur. She needed to look through her sent mail folder to remember how many emails she had written to potential back-end programmers that day.

"Computer programmers are a strange breed," she mused, as she recalled the few uncomfortable phone conversations throughout the day. Just as her stomach began to rumble, she remembered her dinner date with Mom and happily shut down the computer and turned towards the telephone.

"Hi mom, it's already 8 PM," she sighed, looking for sympathy. "I am finally finishing up here. Where should we get dinner?"

It emerged the same question every time, and still, they could never make a quick decision. Finally, both settled on Taverna Opa, the Greek place that always appeared way too loud and hectic but had delicious, garlicky food.

She couldn't exit the office building quickly enough.

The waiters smashed plates on the floor, and electronic dance music blared in the background. Her mom leaned across the table to scream a few words in Faith's ear.

"That lamb ended up excellent! But I can't hear a damn thing!"

She laughed but honestly didn't mind all the noise.
She seemed too tired to make conversation anyway.
Plus, the wine had numbed her brain.
"Are you going out tonight?"
"Yeah, Mom," she yelled, "Dawn should be calling me
in an hour or so. She wants to go down to the beach. I
would rather sleep, but I promised her two days
ago..."
"Poor baby, with the busy social calendar," her mom
teased.

Two hours later, she did burping up garlic in her long,
steamy shower. Every time she closed her eyes, she
saw Mono's smiling face.
"Dammit," she said to herself, "why do you always
have to get yourself into this shit!"
She could picture exactly how he would react to that
question. He would make his most innocent baby
face, with big round blue eyes that would soften
anyone's, heart. But he remained far from a baby and
far from innocent as well. It arose why she had fallen
so hard for him in the first place.
Dawn showed up at 00:30 am, over a half-hour late
like always. And as usual, she began to apply her
makeup in the big mirror while Faith mixed two Stoli
dirty martinis.
"Extra dirty," she teased, "just like you like it, Dawn."

They downed the drinks and hurried downstairs. With a twenty-minute drive ahead of them, it was getting late.

The MacArthur Causeway is one of Miami's most beautiful stretches of road, with the neon lights from the downtown skyscrapers glimmering across the black waters of Biscayne Bay. But on a Thursday night, it seemed the worst place in the city to be. Traffic was hell, although not as bad as L.A.

After parking the car, the girls went straight to Blue, their favorite bar, to start out the night. There, both grooved to the house music and met up with some old high school friends. A few drinks and shots later, the tiny bar packed, and they all needed some fresh air. The walk down Washington Avenue continued to be fun for the Miami natives. Yellow Ferraris cruised by, blasting hip-hop, while the dudes inside the cars yelled out to the drunk girls stumbling along the sidewalk.

"Dude," Dawn yelled, "I can't handle this. I need to dance. Let's just go back up the street to Crowbar. The DJ tonight is good."

She let her lead the way, and they closed the club down at 5 in the morning. On the way out, they wandered next door for a huge, square slice from Pizza Rustica. The best on the beach, Faith claimed, although anything tasted great at that hour.

"You okay to drive?" Dawn mumbled with her mouth full of cheese.

"Yeah," she answered, "let's get the hell out of here. I'm so over South Beach."

Even after chugging two liters of waters before bed, Faith awoke to drums pounding in her head. She swallowed two Excedrin tablets and jumped back under the covers until the pain faded away.
The caffeinated pills worked their magic, and in less than an hour and a half, she appeared to walk into the office, Starbucks in hand.
She mechanically turned on the computer and clicked on the Outlook Express icon. An extensive list of new emails scrolled onto the screen, and she smiled in relief when she saw his email address pop up among the list of senders.
His email occurred short and to the point, like usual.
"I spoke with Tabitha's mother and asked why she had canceled the meeting. She said someone from my office had called her to skip the whole thing to another date. The police are checking on the number already."
He said that he seemed safe and busy at the office.
"The question is for me how these gangsters could know that Mono would be at the office at this time alone," she spoke to herself.
She reread the last words of his mail ten more times before closing the window.
"It's gonna be alright. I love you."
With every re-read, a new smile crept across her face.

She continued filled with a new sense of determination and made a firm decision to move forward with the website. She would hire Bartsoft, the backend programmer company working out of Mississauga, Canada. Working on the Internet allowed her total freedom from the boundaries of office walls. She could hire and oversee employees just about anywhere in the world. The world seemed to brim with brilliant but unemployed techies who acted willingly to work for twenty bucks an hour. After a long and confusing conversation, she and Alex, the owner of Bartsoft finally arrived at an agreement. The project would be rather expensive, but he sounded like he knew his shit. She, on the other hand, acted drowning in a pool of unfamiliar terms and expressions. But she had rehearsed her lines and knew what to ask.

"Look," she explained, "your primary job will be to use PHP for connecting the new HTML interface to an existing MySQL database. But I also need you to create a content management system for our database of albums, and configure the template page for multi-level user access."

"Sure," Alex answered, confident.

They talked money one last time, repeating the amounts just to make everything clear. Alex would send her a PayPal request within the next hour.

She exhaled for the first time only after the phone located back on the cradle. Immediately, she began to write an update email to Mono. The project would take less than twelve months to complete; she wrote but would start when we delivered the website specification along the first HTML pages. Bartsoft would do the work for thirty an hour, transparent and fast, and it seemed worth the cash.

She didn't need to justify her business decisions but added the last line only to rationalize the decision herself. Mono trusted her opinion in all matters and emphasized the fact in all discussions of activity.

After lunch, Faith happened to be surfing the Internet while fighting waves of nausea from one too many cheap vodka-tonics. Cheap booze, she thought to herself, but still ten bucks a pop at the bar.

She clicked through the BoaDaNoite website to catch up on the nightlife in Rio de Janeiro when the telephone ringing broke her concentration. Mono had received her email, and his voice was loud and excited.

"Faith," he exclaimed, "you are the best!

Mono acted still grinning from ear to ear after the phone call ended and Olga appeared standing in front of his desk.

"You beckoned?" she teased.

Olga seemed not the only one to notice the change in her boss's attitude since his last trip to Brazil. This Faith girl must be amazing to have such an intense effect on you, she thought.

Friends always surrounded Mono and, more often than not, the life of the party, but he rarely let anyone in close enough to leave a mark. His conspiratorial attitude emerged his trademark ever since leaving his native East Germany at a young age.

"We need to set up a meeting for you, Jo and me, first thing tomorrow morning. I want to see both of you here, in my office, at 9 AM. It is important, okay?"

Olga could see something did going on but acted afraid to ask. His smile seemed gone, and an intense aura surrounded him. She decided to wait until the next day to find out the whole story.

"Okay, I will call Jo on his cellular and make sure he is here. Is there anything else you need me to do?"

"It's all good. Enjoy your evening, Olga."

Finally, he stayed alone with his thoughts again. Should he confront his people with the ugly truth? Mono decided first to fill up a huge glass with Vodka. He chucked it in one single gulp.

No decision made, but he felt much better after the drink. Mono continued determined to trust in "our force" and see what life has to offer next morning. He remained sure the sun would be shining again. Mono went up to his part of the house and straight to bed without any further thought about anything.

Konninginedag is the day the Dutch citizens reflect unity and togetherness among people in the Netherlands.

Mono continued standing in front of his huge office window watching the preparation for this day on Weteringsschans.

It seemed everyone in the city wanted to create a booth to sell something to the countless tourists would soon pack the streets for the party. All areas of the sidewalk appeared already marked and divided by vendors.

He spoke to himself, "it's like in real life; everyone is marking his territory."

Mono couldn't feel the same happiness in Amsterdam at the moment. Just working and sticking to the plan occurred to be the only option.

"Are you already planning your party weekend?" Olga interrupted the thoughts from inside the office.

"It's nice to have all of it so close. People from all over the world are coming for this weekend to Amsterdam, and we are so privileged to have all the party in walking distance around here. I love the party attitude from the people here so much. What time is it Olga, by the way?"

"It's time for you to put your things together. The entertainment lawyers will be here soon."

"I am ready, don't worry about it."

"Will we go to court with Peter?"

"What do you think?"

"We should fight against it. We paid the advance payment to Eric; another assertion is a lie."

"I agree, but it will be a very costly venture for us with an unknown ending. And you know it's not Peter who canceled the contract. Eric Nouhan continues our contract partner."
"Come on, we all know it's Peter behind it."
"Yes, sure we do. But it doesn't change the fact that our contract partner is Eric.
Honestly, I feel sadly for him."
"Um, Mono, why that?"
"Don't you feel the same way? Eric just had a tour in Australia together with his dancers. Onno and Tal did an outstanding job creating a strong image, super cool designs for the whole album. Eric's face appeared all over in the Netherlands. We inspired people. It's just such a great album. It's such a waste I can only be sad about it. Look at this album, listen to the music. Fans love it!"
Mono dramatically lifted up his right arm, holding the CD between his fingers.
"How beautiful and unique continued to be this work!"
"I agree with you on these issues. Is there no way for you to talk to Eric anymore about it? I mean, it seemed you guys had a good relationship."
"I spoke with his girlfriend Wendy the other day. She is a lovely person and supports the view of our side; Eric is still my friend of course. There are likely deeper forces in play here as well.
I believe he doesn't have the power to resist Peter.
And don't forget with their new production, both will have a hit together, I am sure about it."
"I still don't understand. What seemed to be Peter's incentive?

"You can figure out to justify anything. I stole this one from Samuel Witwer, but it's true.
Peter called me a few weeks ago and asked me if we could hold the release of the Eric Nouhan "Magic Inspiration" album back for two weeks. A song he produced together with Eric appeared on our album as you know.
He wanted to have the songs single CD in the store first."
"This remained the reason why we rescheduled the release?"
"Yes, therefore our entire swindle to Free Record. Anyway, last week Peter saw our album at Outland Records on sale. He made a big scene there, so the manager from the store called me."
"What happened to be Peter's problem?"
"Peter acted super upset because we released "Magic Inspiration" without checking with him first."
"He got what he asks for, two weeks. We updated our printed back cover three times because he kept changing the name of the song, remember? His song is exclusive with Eric Nouhan on our album. It's just ridiculing."
Mono stood up from his chair and walked over to the CD player. "Where is the "Zenith" promo CD Olga? Deep Zone - "It's Gonna Be Allright" started hitting in the room.

Mono went on. "Of course I remember. We paid the bills for it. Exclusive, this is the point. Peter is trying to get out of the deal by manipulating Eric because it's not a good one for him. He looks stupid. Peter is aware of it since Radio 538 asked RW Records for the non-exclusive license of the song. Peter is for some odd reason in competition with me."
"You believe his motives are going this deep?"
"I believe they are going even deeper than that."
"What are you talking about?"
"At the "Energy Hours" party last week, Peter acted totally rude. He approached me and said, "I will fuck you up, and show how things are done in this city now. I forbid you to use my logo any longer for your label advertising campaign"."
"You didn't tell me why?"
"I don't want to worry you."
The buzzing phone interrupted the end of the explanations.
"Olga responds please," Mono asked, exasperated. "I am not here."
Olga walked to a corner of the room and returned a few minutes later to finish the conversation.
"What's up?" he asked.
"It's the law office. They want to move our appointment to Tuesday, 2 pm at the lawyer's office.
"That's fine with me."

"RW Record's will lose a lot of investment and most importantly credit," Olga continued.

"Eric's lawyer's letter to RW Records said that it is forbidden for us to sell and or license the record. The record is already on sale, and we will do shit to stop that. I don't see any reason for us to waste our time worrying. We will license the album not today or tomorrow but one day we will again. For now, we will sell the units we have. Our dreams are in full force."

"We will ship the latest order of "Magic Inspiration" to Australia?"

"Sure we will. I don't believe Peter will invest a lot of money in this lawyer thing for Eric. He just wants to correct his error and control the situation, showing his power in the city."

"I see it different, Mono. It seems to me; he wants to put RW Records in financial difficulties to control our operations."

"You don't know a person's character until the cards are down*. Peter seems a sick man capable of a lot of shit. You should be aware better than I do."

"Tell me about it," she murmured.

Mono continued. "It's all about the big picture, timing, being a step ahead of our competition, tenacity despite failure in between and having some fun & parties along the way*." Mono became aware of his rising voice, and he took a deep breath.

Olga shook her head. "I am a native boss. I grew up in Amsterdam. It is just the beginning. It isn't aimed against the record only; it's aimed at our whole project."

Mono agreed to listen to Olga's opinion.

"You have a point. Anyway, Olga, we have a plan, it's late, and you should get going. It's party time."
"There is no way I am leaving now! I am enjoying our conversation way too much right now. I finally get a chance to see deeper into your soul."
"Hahaha," he cackled. "Look at the sun and the happy people outside. You should get mixed up with them."
"No way!" she insisted. Olga pressed on.
"Will Faith be with you together in Ibiza?"
She is busy with her university applications over the summer and will stay in Miami."
Do you already have the date of your departure in mind?"
"It depends on the "Hot Weekend Amsterdam" records and Tabitha's new single CD. Jo said both would be ready for pick up in Hilversum in three weeks' time. I will leave when I hold the first CD boxes in my hand."
"Does that mean we won't see you here the entire summer?
"Maybe I come back when Unlimited Ways is shooting Tabitha's new clip, but I am not sure. Those guys are pros; all set, so I don't need to be around."
"What we will do all of the time without you?" Olga cried. "We need you!"
"Olga, come on. You need to put in all of your efforts in the "Zenith Pacha" album project. We have a deadline to keep. My place is in Ibiza this summer."
"Why are you teasing me?" she whined. "I am young but you know I have headhunters breathing down my neck. Be careful, or I may take one of them up on their offers!"

Mono smirked.
"There is something I wanted to tell you after the weekend only."
"What is it?"
"We will throw two parties this summer on the island."
"Are you kidding?"
"I am not. The dates confirmed with Amnesia and Space. DJs are confirmed as well."
"How long have you known this?
He checked his watch.
"Since about two hours, Olga. We will have a release party for the "Hot Weekend Amsterdam" records July, 31 at Amnesia. And at the end of the summer, a "Fly with us" after hour party at Space."
"I knew you seemed cooking up something boss, I speak little German and wanted or not I understood enough of your conversations with your friend Iris to get a clue about it. Who arranged all of it?"
"Haha, I knew you would Olga. Mirko from Ibiza Dance Promotion made it happen. Do you remember the producer?"
"Of course I do. Mirko is the guy from Chile, right? I met him at the Tribe "Ibiza Reunion" party at Escape?"
"Yep, you did."
"What about the crew, Tabitha, The Funky Fakirs, Onno, Tal, Jo, Sebastian, Robby, Toffy, Angela, and Sanni? Do any of them know about it yet? I am just so excited about it."
"Not yet, of course. But the whole crew will be on these dates in Ibiza as well!"

"Which DJs are on the list? Mono put on his thinking face. "The Funky Fakirs, of course, Tom Harding, Mark Spoon but with a question mark, Commander Tom, Carlos Diaz, Tofke, Voodoo plus Space and Amnesia residents."
"Please tell me your secret."
"I just keep my mind busy with positive thoughts. It's easy, you should give it a try," Mono said with a smile on his face. "But I am sure your excitement will disappear suddenly, Olga, when you realize that you will have to coordinate most of the work from the office in advance, plus all of the contract obligations we have towards ID&T in the Netherlands."
"Oh, you can be sure it will be my pleasure. Amsterdam is not the worse place to work anyway."
"I am glad to hear it, Olga."
The grin on his face appeared even bigger now.
Olga continued still a bit frustrated, however.
"I just wish I could read your mind a little bit."
"Stand in line, Olga. Now get out of here. Next week will be a hard week again, and I have had enough of work for this week. You can let yourself out. I will leave for Rokerij. I need a joint urgently. Goodbye!"
"Hold on Mono. There is something Jo and I wanted to tell you, also after the weekend only."
"Ok, I am listening now."
"Micha Klein will create the artwork for Tabitha's print advertising campaign, and Roberto called they would throw release parties for the "Zenith Pacha" album in Ibiza at the end of the season and another at Le Prince Club Elysees in Paris at the beginning of November."

"This is excellent. I am proud of you guys. Have a lovely "Queen's Day" weekend."
"The same for you, Boss."
All of a sudden Olga appeared alone in the office. She could picture all of the exciting work for the summer in her mind already. She called her sister to tell her all summer plans have changed.

The first day of the fall brought bright sun to Amsterdam. Third Bass - "N.Y. Groove" happened to beat from the stereo in the office. Olga and Jo exchanged stories from the past summer on the island. They both agreed on the company parties at Amnesia, Space seemed a highlight, but the people, beaches, and trips with the companies' Tullio Abbate offshore boat appeared to be the hit after all and a lot of fun. All of the sudden Jo changed the subject.
"Do you go with Mono to Paris for the "Zenith Pacha" release party?"
"I have been for the party at Pacha past week this time you will go, Jo. I spoke with Mono already about it, he agreed, and it's fine with him. By the way, when Sentinel will have the new CDs ready for pick-up?"
Jo had a bright grin on his face listening to the good news.
"At the end of October, the reprint will have the year on the cover as Mono had wished a few weeks ago. Ono sent the new design all ready to Hilversum."
"Isn't it a bit late end of October?"

"We still have enough units in stock to satisfy the demands in the Netherlands. For the party in Paris, we have a ten-day window, more than enough time. Something else is bothering me much more. We are not working on something new here in Amsterdam anymore. Before Mono left for Ibiza, he stuck around with DJ Peran all of the time. We all know both are working on a record together. He isn't telling us anything about his new plans. Don't you realize it?"
"Did he confirm to you that he is producing a record with Peran together?"
"Mono acted not hiding the phone conversations with Faith at the office, but officially he told me nothing about it." "Mono spoke about the Ramin Project trance song plan with us, Jo. RW Records will be present at the first Amsterdam Dance Event in two weeks' time. Tabitha has gigs all over the place and some radio interviews at local stations starting next week, it is more than doing nothing, " "do you remember the conversation we had with Mono in the spring after all of the problems had accumulated?"
"I recall every word good I acted speechless the whole day hearing all of the facts. I had hoped after our recent advertising campaign in Holland, our super summer in Ibiza and the successful Popkomm music fair in Cologne he changed his tactics."
Natural Born Grooves - "Groovebird" happen to be pounding from the stereo in the room.
Don't be naive Jo. Mono will be gone rather sooner than later. I asked him about it before I left Ibiza last week. He answered me with a riddle, and he refused to explain anything more."
"What did he say to you tell me please?"

"Mono said: "'our force" planted "our plant," the people will pour the required waters. We need to leave to protect the grow up. When she is mature, we are back, to claim the clone. Then the time is on.'"
Jo wrote it down on a piece of paper and appeared shaking his head.

"Time is nothing; timing is everything," Mono recounted to himself, experiencing challenging events, together with "our force" that time. Sequential - "Trip to Paradise" continued to beat in his earphones.

Mono arrived in Sao Paulo at the time the Brazilian metrological summer did just start, feeling excited to be back.
Thomas stood to wait in front of the international passenger exit at Guarulhos.
Thomas saw him as he walked through the exit door, but Mono continued too busy to notice. He stowed away his passport at his jacket pockets after he looked up and saw Thomas walking in his direction. They greeted each other like friends who hadn't seen each other for a quite a while.
Thomas smiled and opened the conversation.

"You look triumphal."
"I am. It is always nice to be here, and especially for the occasion. How is your wife doing?"
"She is doing fine and is busy in our office. She sends you welcome greetings. Let's walk to my car. I have a guy waiting there who is curious to welcome you as well."
"Now I am curious. Who is it?"
"I promised him not to tell you. He wants to see if you recognize him. Look, we are already there." Thomas pointed with his right hand to a parking lot.
"I know that guy. He happened to be my first guide in Sao Paulo" Mono said hesitantly.
"Hold on. Yashin is his name. What is he doing here with you?"
"Yashin started working for MBB. He is our record promotion manager."
"That's an excellent choice, Thomas. I like your pick." Mono and Yashin hugged each other.
"What a small world, man. How are you doing Yashin?"
"I am good, man," he answered. "Give me your bag I will put it in the trunk."
"Let's sit together in the back seat," Thomas suggested.
"Like VIPs," Mono smiled. "I like it."
Yashin the Brazilian connector began driving towards Jardins.
"Hot Weekend Amsterdam" - CD one appeared streaming from the car CD sound system. Mono recognized The Funky Fakirs intro instantly and looked directing with his right hand.

Thomas quickly asked, "Where is Faith? Is she not coming to Brazil?"

"Faith has been in Rio de Janeiro for a few days already."

"Why didn't you guys travel together?"

"That happened to be the plan, but I came from LA, as I had to stay longer than expected there. Susanne Rau from Universal Music Germany visited me for few days."

"That's very exciting, a long way to a meeting."

"It surely seems that way. My friend Ramin made the connection. It seemed they had some interests in our trance-record project."

"Did you reveal our plan to the manager?" "Steve Castro provided a VIP service for her, and we showed her around at Steve's & TJ's parties in town, in the final, she seemed not convinced about our project. I revealed the target; I guess it killed the interests. I suppose she had marked me insane. Faith decided to go as originally planned. I will travel tomorrow to Rio de Janeiro. Anyway, do we have any new knowledge regarding our list?"

"Sure, I would say we have very satisfying news. We got the license confirmation from Black Hole Recordings yesterday. DJ Tiesto, Ralphie B and Midway are officially on our track-list now."

Mono grinned widely.

"DJ Tiesto can tear down the wall. Congrats."

"That's not all," Thomas continued. "MBB made a pre-deal with FNAC. They will sell the album in all stores in Sao Paulo."

Yashin seemed especially happy about the DJ Tiesto news. He continued to be a big fan of his music.

Thomas interrupted Yashin's celebration in the driver seat.

"Keep on driving, Yashin."

"Thomas let him celebrate, makes me happy too. Let me asked you a question. We are missing still confirmation from Vandit Records, Discomania, Spinnin Records, ID&T and Media Records, right?"

"This is correct."

"March 15 is our deadline for all licensing confirmed, shall I be worried?"

"It's just a time issue, but maybe the time limit is too tight. April 15 would be safe."

"Thomas this doesn't work for us. Failing our deadline would put at risk our plan."

"I need the master only by April 25 in Sao Paulo. You shouldn't worry so much."

"We invited DJ Peran to a short vacation in Rio for the Easter Holidays. He is arriving on March 27. He wants to bring the master recording with him. You see my dilemma?"

"Very clear my friend. I see it very clear. We will do our best to make your deadline happen."

"Thank you so much, Thomas."

"Make a layover on your way out of Brazil. Adriana wants to invite you guys to our home for a dinner or lunch again."

"Sure, we will do that. We stay in touch closely anyway. I guess we will be in Rio until April 19. Faith will leave maybe for the WMC in Miami a month earlier, but this isn't sure. Let's hope everything goes smoothly. Yashin, please stop on the corner Alameida Santos and Rua Augusta. I need an ATM. Give me five, Thomas. It is all cool. Give our greetings to Adriana. And it was nice seeing you again, Yashin."

In Mono's apartment, he dialed Faith's number in Rio.
"I am in Sao Paolo, honey."
"Oh, there you are. I did start to wonder because on the website it said the flight continued on time."
"The trip went fine, except that the 5-hour stopover in Miami occurred to be horrible."
Sonic INC – "I feel 4 you" – Taste of Summer – Fire and Ice Vital - Remix played at his place from the stereo.
"Why didn't you call Gene? You guys could have met for dinner."
"I thought about it, but I didn't want to bother him.
"It's fine, I guess. Is everything alright in LA?"
"All went perfectly."
"Will you see Thomas tomorrow morning?"
"He updated me already, on the ride from the airport to my place. I will rent a car tomorrow morning, and in the afternoon, I will leave Sao Paulo."
"Do you have any good news from Thomas?"

"We could run into more trouble. We will talk about it when I am in Rio. I am super tired, honey, I need some sleep."
"Okay, honey. I love you."
"Love you too."
"I have one more thing Mono!"
"What is it what you want?"
"Please be carefully tonight in Sao Paulo. I know you, and I don't want you to get in trouble, okay? I want you here in Rio in one piece tomorrow."
"Of course, honey, I won't do anything crazy."
Right after the conversation had ended; he picked up the phone right away again and dialed his ex-wife's number in Germany. Christine, the beautiful Greeks ex-model, remained famous for being a late bird. This time the plan didn't work her mother answered, and Mono hung up the phone without even talk to her. A happy flashback appeared in his brain doing "the party" with Christina, celebrating life together with all friends at the first DT 64 - "Mayday" party in Berlin - Weissensee 1991.
Undecided, Mono sat in front of his TV jumping through the channels, controlling the remote in his right hand. Nothing exiting appeared, so he took his clothes off and went to his bathroom. The shower had a stimulating effect on him. For a second, he considered calling his friend DJ Alex, but decided against it and went to sleep instead.

It appeared to be already dark outside when he woke up again. The usual cacophony from the street had already disappeared. He went straight to his wardrobe to check for clothes he could wear for the night.

"There you are," he thought.

He found his long-lost Calvin Klein jeans. Seconds later, he jumped into his jeans, put on a white shirt and went again to his bathroom. He used some of his favorite "Michael" perfume and decided that only brushing his teeth would do it for the night. His stomach acted growling for food while he continued checking his face in the mirror. He seemed happy with what he saw.

"Tonight is a good night for Love Story," Mono mused. It happens to be the most famous hot girl club in the city. Twenty minutes later he appeared sitting at Habib's on Rua Augusta, eating his favorite fast food in Brazil, Charuto Repolho and "Bib'sFiha" de Frango using a lot of spice.

Love Story occurred to be in walking distance from Rua Augusta. It is a paradise for guys and girls who want to get laid for a night. Mainly foreign businesspeople showed up to the party most of the time. He liked the Disco. The electronic dance music continued pumping when he entered the room. He thought for a second, wow, cool, Westbam – hard trance kicking. The place packed as always. At the last moment, he changed his order to a straight Cachaça, one of his favorites. Something for a real man, he remained telling. The drink burned his mouth like a habanero pepper. He knew he would regret the drink decision the next morning.

The next day late in the afternoon Mono arrived at Rua Moreira Neves, West Zone of Rio de Janeiro. A recently-developed upscale neighborhood with almost no skyscrapers in sight, the area contained a lot of hills, little lakes and jungles, all sorts of tropical fruits and different animals as alligators, snakes and his favorite beast Capivara.

Andrea, the building's caretaker, appeared the first one to welcome him home. They both shared passion - the love for the CR Flamengo soccer team. After the exchange of some kindnesses, Mono went up to the second floor to his apartment.

He could already smell in the hallway that something delicious seemed waiting for him.

A little moment later he opened the door and entered holding Faith firm in his arms. The couple' could feel the energy circulating through both bodies as a power circuit. She had her Faith smile on her face. Their lips touched each other without any movement for a while. The lovers' looked into each other's eyes. It meant more than exchanging words. It felt wonderful to be together again.

"Guys, vamos, the foods are getting cold."

Wuffi continued making his point and interrupting the ceremony.

He appeared to walk on his way to the terrace with some plates in his right hand and a huge bowl in his left hand. Mono managed somehow to give him a quick hug.

"Hi, Wuff, Peran sends you greetings!"

His only response, "take care, it's hot."

Mono smiles about it as usual.

Wuffi acted always dramatically stressed out after he had cooked meal. He seemed only happy again when everyone appeared eating around the table.
The couple' arrived at the dinner table immediately after Wuffi began serving the food.
Both respected his ceremony, and neither of them spoke a word.
After a few bites, Wuffi began the conversation by explaining the recipes for his meal.
"Your turkey is the best, my friend. The potato puree with gravy on top is a hit. Did you make the puree with sour cream?
"Of course man only handmade cream."
"Taste the red cabbage mhmm!"
Faith seemed in love with the food.
After ten minutes, Wuffi had already finished two plates. Like always, he left the table mumbling his usual excuses.
Both acted smiling about it.
"I am so stuffed."
Faith folded her hands over her stomach together. She got comfortable in her chair.
"Are you happy to be back?"
He cleaned his mouth with a napkin.
"Sure I am." He tossed the napkin onto the table.
"My ticket occurred to be a last minute business in LA. I cashed a check at a US Bank from Castro Enterprises to pay for my ticket, while Anthony booked my flight at a travel agency in Studio City, four hours before my departure. The connection flight left Miami the same time my maximum stay in the U.S. expired."

"I am happy; I will not worry anymore. Everything is alright. It is the most important thing. You made it."
"Yes, I did. Let me get comfortable and later let's go for a walk to the beach. What do you think, Faith?"
"I will clean up the table. Give me fifteen minutes."

It looked to be a rainy but summer evening. Both appeared to walk towards the beach, passing along the Chico Mendes Park sidewalk until they took a left on Gilka Machado. The road led straight to the Canto do Recreio. A huge rock marked the end of Recreio Beach on one side and the beginning of Macumba Beach on the other. Both are major surfing spots in this region.
"Do you want to have a beer? I will buy," Faith offered.
"Sounds like a plan. Where we should go?"
"What about Mauricio's kiosk on the beach?"
"This is a perfect choice."
Mono picked out a table where they had an excellent view of the ocean. Faith came back with two cans of Itaipava in her hands.
The beer appeared extra cold, as always in Brazil.
"Prost Faith."
"Prost Mono."
"We have few months of precious time together; can you believe this, Faith?

"Honestly I am getting used to this idea," she said smiling. "Do you want to talk a little about business? Thomas sent me an email with a protocol about your meeting with him yesterday."
"Sure I do. What do you think about it?"
"It's obvious we are approaching a vital stage of our project. Thomas says he is running out of his resources. We owe Thomas already. The licenses are getting expensive because the Real is down vs. the Dollar."
"I know the exchange rate is shitty for him right now. I am not worried - he knows what he is doing."
"I agree with you. But we need a financial plan b in case something goes wrong."
"We could transfer to him some pre-album sales money from America."
"As a Plan C, yes, but I wouldn't do it before all of the licenses are confirmed."
"We need to use our resources if necessary?"
"Vanessa the Australian model told me a while ago that she has some potential backers in line in Amsterdam. Let me call her tomorrow."
"We can transfer funds immediately in case Thomas is in urgent need," "let us see what happens. Time for another round of beer! Hold on; I will get it."
Faith watched Rodrigo Negao, a local skate hero doing his fancy tricks on the sidewalk of the beach promenade.
"Did you make an itinerary for our time here?" Mono asked.
"We should try to work at least 6 hours a day. It's hard enough in this crazy heat, though."

"Yeah, it will not be so easy to stay focused here, but we have no choice. We need to keep going. Internet speed is a big problem. Here are only a few places around with any high-speed connection."
"Tell me about it. I went to Copacabana this morning. I just happened to be sick of our shitty dial up connection. Anyway, we are now on a hold. Let's work on our plan execution; it's all MBB for now."
"Peran could spend a lot of time to record the master for nothing; we still don't know if we get all tracks licensed by our deadline."
"Don't worry trust in "our force." Let's start heading towards home. I have a surprise for you."
"What is it?"
"Wait until we are home." she said with a giant grin on her face.

Faith entered the living room asking Mono.
"Who are you talking to?"
"Just on a sec honey," "bye brother is was nice talking to you again."
"It happened to be DJ Lex on the phone. He asked me if we make it for the Ultra Music Festival this year. The festival isn't anymore in South Beach?"
"It's in Bayfront Park since last year already. What you answered him?"
"I told him that you could maybe be there for the WMC but not me. Call him after you are back anyway."

"I will do that for sure. Let's go down to Ipanema I want some street carnival today, and on the way home tonight we make a stop in Barra. We can't miss the DJ set from Carl Cox tonight. It is a must go."
"This sounds like an excellent plan to me. I will call a ride for us."

Peran van Dijk the Dutch producer came from Amsterdam via Paris to Rio de Janeiro.
The information board reported the landing of flight 649.
"You need to hear it!"
Peran shouted, while he exited the baggage area, and walked straight towards Faith and Mono, catching the attention of curious onlookers.
Peran arrived hugging both together.
"Guys, guys, listen! I stayed working on the music until the last minute. I almost missed my flight. You need to hear my wild story."
Faith tried to convince DJ Peran to be patient.
"Hold your tale until we are home, Peran. Wuffi cooked for you."
"A delicious veggie dinner Perani," Mono urged, using one his nicknames for the DJ.
DJ Peran gave up finally.
"Okay guys, I can wait one more hour but...."
The couple' acted both laughing because DJ Peran appeared ready for his next attempt to tell the hot story.

It seemed to be a half hour drive from the International Airport to Leme on a superb day. There the couple' had rented an apartment right in front of the beach for DJ Peran.
Wuff welcomed them with the same meal procedure as always. DJ Peran barely had a chance to say hello to him.
"Where is my room? Wow, this place is huge. Look there is the beach! I need to go for a walk soon."
"Help yourself, Peran, the place is all yours. Wuff will stay with you for the next week. You have two more rooms to choose. Is that enough?" Faith wanted to know.
"This is fantastic! Thank you so much. I just can't understand why you guys moved to Recreio. South Zone is beautiful, always."
"Recreio is a real paradise, with the most fantastic beaches of Rio de Janeiro. Come to see the sunrise, the surfers...everything. You will love it," Mono tried to convince the DJ.

A little later on the dinner table, Peran eagerly slurped down his third bowl of soup.
"Oh Wuff, I love your veggie soups. No one in the whole world makes them like you."
DJ Peran appeared in love with Wuff's food.
Wuff answered, smiling, "you are very welcome........"
Peran cleaned up his mouth and put the napkin on his plate and went on.

"Okay, here it comes my tragic story guys, sixty minutes before my departure from Amsterdam; I stayed still working on our album at the Bunker Studio in Hilversum. Can you believe this? He looked over in Mono's direction, waiting for a reaction. Mono responded shaking his head in disbelief waiting for the good news. Peran went on.

"Twenty miles away from the airport, rush hour time, stop and go. Racing slalom in direction airport in the forbidden lane, listening to our mix, calling a friend to make arrangements to pick up my car, dropping the car right in front of departures, hiding my keys inside, running to the gate in need of a miracle imagine?"

Peran stopped talking all of the sudden, watching in the round. Not one said a word.

"I tried hard, but I couldn't finish all work in time." It emerged an unpleasant moment, everyone acted speechlessly and looking in Peran's direction......searching for a sign of hope. No one could see anything until Peran continued smiling.

"But here it is our treasure," waving the CD in the air. All were jumping, euphoric and clapping hands, shouting, "Peran, Peran, Peran."

It happened to be one of the many gorgeous days in Rio de Janeiro. The sun appeared shining, and the sky seemed Rio blue.

Faith and Mono obligated to be working at home. A light wind made it tolerable, sitting outside on the terrace. DJ Tiesto -"Suburban Train" - Amsterdamcing Mix continued going from the stereo sound system. Peran had already left the city for Los Angeles, and Wuff did visit Vanessa in Sidney.

Faith closed her laptop and dropped it on a small wooden table nearby. She appeared to be in a mood of a conversation.

"You know DJ Tiesto shall be our magic DJ since when?"

Mono closed his laptop watching in Faith direction only to put up a thoughtful face; Mono slowly began talking. "Well, we never met in person.........," "I got a DJ Tiesto cassette mixtape early in 1996 from my scene scout in the Netherlands. The tape inspired me very much. I hadn't had this feeling for years. I began to follow him right away over the years. Since the ID&T "Sensation" party at the Amsterdam Arena two years ago I am sure. His magic convinced me. DJ Tiesto played a sensational set." Mono left the patio. After ten minutes he appeared again holding three VHS tapes in his hand.

"Let's watch the whole show. It's amazing what happened in the Netherlands about trance music. Time passed by and all we wanted to happen all of the sudden appeared in all forms."

"I have seen the tapes Mono. It's fascinating indeed." Mono kept insisting watching at least some scenes of the show. Faith had different intentions at this moment. She kept pushing the issue.

"You never considered a German DJ could be the right one for our American journey?" "Of course we thought it. DJ Dag, the master who inspired "our force," could have been the one; unfortunately for us, he had other life plans. We never had a possibility to talk to him about it. He remains around and produces magic for the fans. Our friend Mark Spoon has it in him. I tried to talk to him about it, though. Vanessa went to Mark's birthday party at the Dorian Gray in Frankfurt/Main 3 years ago, with two limos and 15 supermodel friends in tow for additional help, to convince him to experience the project with us together. He is living the Rockstar life in Germany. We never got a chance. Our dear friend Iris tried to convince him as well but without success. Mark Spoon invited me to the "German Dance Awards" show in Hamburg two years ago. He told me on the occasion that he supports our project anywhere he can anyway. It occurred to be good enough for me. Paul van Dyk is German and has enormous potential, but his spirits as a live DJ aren't convincing me. His management seems little open to adventures. So far as I can tell at least. I can't feel with him what I need to sense. Still, he makes my top five of course." "I understand what you are talking about." "Well, here is another German I assumed it before, DJ Taucher. Wagges, Christina and I appeared chatting in front of Wuff's club in Lampertheim, late in the afternoon one day. All super high on XTC, as usual, those days. A ghostly guy, with a facemask, wearing construction worker clothes including helmet, accompanied by a man in a diving suit including dive mask, carrying a huge Stofftier and a little green carpet, approached us. The masked man said, 'Hi, I am Koma, and this guy here is my friend Taucher we want to be DJs. Help us out please.' Imagine this fucking hilarious scene. We all felt it instantly. We arranged for Taucher & Koma a gig at Wuff's "Marilyn - After Hours" party back in the November of 1991. It happened to be super cool, a lot of fun and good music. 24 hour nonstop dancing; at this day "our force" emerged cloned for the first time. Both began throwing parties together. It seemed a fast success story. A little time later the couple' split and the clone disappeared. DJ Taucher continues to be present and marvelous."

"I like the stories I get your point."

"I am happy you do. Wagges and I we both knew we needed a lot of patience to create our environment, to begin with, our challenging project.

At our last meeting about it, before Wagges deceased, we decided that we will plant "our plant" in Amsterdam. The present of the story you know."

"Why the Netherlands there are plenty of choices around?"

"I had previous experiences in a market of the size of Holland. Plus the Dutch infrastructure provides everything our project needs. It's an obvious choice don't you think so?"

"Are you talking about the vinyl mail order you owned together with your friends Bio and Walter in East Germany?"

"You remember the story that's very impressive Faith."

"How Peran came into the picture?"
"Our friend Eelko van Kooten, the co-founder of Spinnin Records, had recommended me. Eelko knew about our project from an earlier stage. I guess he felt I needed a favor. Peran visited me at my office one day and offered me Peran - "Eye of the Tiger" – Trance Remixes for licensing. It happened a few years ago. We became friends. Peran pointed me to - Armin van Buuren, Rank 1, Ralphie B and others and soon became for me the genius of the sounds. He is an excellent DJ as well. His talent makes it work all of the time."
Faith agreed without any but.
"I am glad that Thomas likes the album so much as we do."
"Honestly, Faith, I had no doubts about it. I am just pleased that the master arrived in one piece at his office in Sao Paulo. Let's hope the same will happen with Thomas his shipment to his printing company in the Amazon."
"Hahaha..... You remember, you never know around here. At least we have backups, and Sedex proved it's a company worth the money."
"Yes, the shipment seemed to be not that cheap. I only hope that we will get the missing licenses soon. It's now or never, Faith. We don't have another attempt. I agreed to manage our project back in the summer of 1993. Damn long time has passed since that day. The time is on!"
Mono couldn't hide his worried face.

"Just trust in "our force!" Everything will work out just fine. You know what? We should stop working for the day, drive down to Grumari Beach and get a couple of hours of sun on our pale bodies while watching Junior, Kbleo and Negao Flamenguista surf. I met Kbleo at Tattoo's shop this morning, and he told me they all would be there today late afternoon. What do you think?"
Mono took a deep breath and agreed. "That sounds like a superb idea. We will grab an Acai half-way, at the Prainha Beach at little Gabriel's father's point on."

IX

The Discovery

Faith dialed Mono's number in Rio.

"Hi Honey. I am calling from my apartment."

"Oh, Baby, you made it back safe! It's great to hear your voice. How are you?"

"I am sad, I can't believe how quickly those months passed by, and I am already back here in Miami."

"Sorry, Baby, I am lonely as well. What are your plans for today?"

"Well...", "I guess I will go out for lunch to Bagel Bar with mom. In the evening I will have dinner with Gene and talk with him about the progress of our project."

"By the way, we have good news. I just got a call from Thomas; Armin van Buuren presents Rising Stars - "Clear Blue Moon" and Solid Sleep - "Club Attack" – Paul van Dyk – Remix both confirmed. Don't you have his mail?"

"Let me check for a sec. Oh, yea sorry, I guess I do have of those emails all here in my Inbox, this is excellent news. It's lifting my mood up."

"You know what that means? I will be in Miami on April 19. I will arrive at 7.30 am on a United Airlines flight. How does that sound to you?"

"It looks good to me."

"I will call you later tonight, okay? Love you, honey."

"Love you, too. Sorry, I am out of it. It was a long trip for me."
She hung up the phone a huge smile slowly crept across her face.

Mono walked straight towards of one of the immigration desks that greeted thousands of foreign visitors daily at the Miami International Airport.
"I am back in Miami," Mono thought, and a feeling of relief rushed through him as he walked more quickly. He could already picture Faith outside the north terminal, waiting for him in a parking lot.
The immigration officer checked Mono's passport information more intense than usual. Something appeared obviously different. The guy had no expression on his face. He placed Mono's passport next to his computer.
"Sir, please wait here. An officer will be here shortly."
A few minutes later, he arrived.
Mono's heart began beating hard. Mono tried to keep his cool.
"Please follow me," his firm words to Mono. The men walked, switching corridors few times. The Immigration officer finally stopped in front of a room and opened the door. Pointing to a chair in front of a plain wood table, he barked, "Please sit down. An officer will be with you shortly."

Mono stayed alone with his thoughts for few minutes. He occurred in full consciousness of the gravity of his situation. A flashback of the past appeared in his brain. The moment Wagges convinced him to promote an album with all favorite trance DJs in America. Totally high on XTC sprawling on large chairs on the second-floor terrace of Schaeffler's Casa Del Luz, the holiday paradise in Port D'Es Torrent, listening to a Sven Väth, DJ Dag, and Torsten Fenslau - live set at Hessentag in Lich 1993.

A senior immigration officer entered the room. He held some papers and Mono's passport in his hands.

"Good morning, Sir."

"Good morning what is the problem officer?"

The man flipped through the pages of Mono's passport. "Why has been your US B1 visa application denied?

"The application process couldn't be finished in 48 hours by the consulate in Rio de Janeiro as promised. I asked my passport back because of an already scheduled trip at the time."

The man did not show any reaction.

"Why you haven't been in your home country for such a long time? Do you have problems in Germany? What are you doing in America? Why do you have an American driver license?"

The questions had a sound of accusations.

"I am traveling. I don't have any problem in Germany. I want to visit the United States for pleasure and business. I need the license to drive a car, belong to my business in America."

The officer did not seem convinced by his statement.

"I don't believe a single word you said." "Have you ever been arrested in your life?" Mono felt a bomb just exploded in front of his face.
Mono kept his calm attitude.
"I haven't Sir," Mono answered.
The officer immediately left the room.

It appeared to be now in the afternoon - six hours had passed by without any unusual movement.
Mono could hear steps coming closer in front of the room. He could overhear a conversation between a female officer and his case officer. The door opened a little at this moment. "Do you have an answer from Germany about the guy?"
"We can't find anything on him, although I am pretty sure there is something unusual about him."
"Let him go," occurred the female officer words.
A moment later, his case officer stood in front of him.
"You are free to go. Welcome to America and enjoy your stay here." He stamped his passport and handed him over to Mono.
"Thank you, Sir."
Mono rushed straight towards the baggage area, praying he would be able quickly to locate his luggage. All passengers of his flight had cleared out hours before already.
Mono asked a friendly looking United Airlines hostess, "Where can I find my bags."
"Please give me your boarding card, Sir."

She checked the numbers at her computer terminal. "They are still at customs. Just walk one minute in this direction," pointing with her right hand at the baggage claim exit.

A customs officer appeared already waiting when Mono showed up in front of his desk.
"These are your bags?" The officer asked, pointing at two bags next to his desk.
"Yeah, these are my bags."
"Please open the big bag; I want to have a look. Do you have anything to declare?"
The customs officer dogged through his bag.
"No, Sir."
Mono seemed allowed to go.
Finally, Mono passed by the last door and entered the hallway at the crowded North terminal.
An unwanted sound made his heart freeze.
"Sir, Sir": Mono heard someone shouting. He turned around and saw the very same customs officer walking in his direction. The man stopped right in front of him.
Mono thought he would get a heart attack any moment. A back flash appeared in his brain. He put Wagges favorite music cassette with a recording of the Torsten Fenslau & DJ Dag - live show - Radio HR3 - "Three year's Club Night" on top of his friend's coffin.

"Please come back to my desk please, Sir. I have another question."
Mono followed the officer back to the customs area.
"Interesting day," Mono thought.
"How I can help you, Sir?"
"How much cash do you have on you?"
"$150 in cash and my credit cards just."
The officer seemed relieved for the first time.
"I wish you an excellent time in the United States."
Mono grabbed his bags again and quickly strode out towards the exit, still trying to figure out how he has survived this day.
"I feel it Wagges," Mono said to his friend watching to the roof.
He searched his pockets while a Marlboro Light cancer stick dangled between his lips.
"Where is that stupid cell phone?" searching all of his pockets several times over.

"Where are you? I emerged so worriedly about it. What is going on?"
Faith acted frantic on the other end of the phone line.
"Calm down, honey. I am in front of the North terminal at the Miami airport. I will explain everything to you. Please come and pick me up. I just want to go home."
"I called Immigration, and an officer told me Immigration is holding you back, but nobody would say why."

"Calm down, honey, just pick me up." Faith still seemed outraged, and Mono went on. "Everything will be okay. Quite down, honey, just pick me up."

Twenty-five minutes later, Faith arrived at the airport. Mono appeared waiting on the sidewalk, a cigarette in his mouth. Faith stopped the car, opened the door and jumped into his arms.
"Don't cry. It's all good now."
Kissing and hugging each other with relief.
"Let's start driving, honey. I need a shower and some food."
"We could grab a Burrito on the way to my place. Gene will meet us at New China Buffet in Hallandale for dinner early tonight, so a little snack should be enough for now."
"Sounds like a plan to me,"
"By the way, welcome to Miami." Faith continued. "I still want to know what happened at immigration today."
"Thank you. Immigration kept questioning me, about my denied business visa application that is going on. Let's drive and enjoy the Miami sun".
"I remember the day; I escorted you to the consulate in Rio."
"Yeah that's true, I believe the immigration officer has dogged deep in my records today."
"This occurred to be perfect for you, honey."

"It's not. The immigration officer made an inquiry about me with German authorities; I overheard a conversation between two officers. We are living in strange times."
"You are a free man!"
"It's the second inquiry from the Americans about me in just one year of time. It's a question of days, and U.S. immigration will receive an investigation about my whereabouts in America from German authorities.
"You are paranoid, regarding what; it happened to be different times. Ages ago that you continued a person of interest?"
"The East German Secret Service put me on the watch list when I occurred to be a kid; West German state protection got to hold on some classified files about my activities in East Germany, right before the German reunion. The spooks misused the information. Bad judgment or intentionally, who knows? I have my private thoughts about it. Anyway, I appeared right away on another watch list as a consequence. I have reliable information about it."
"You scare me Mono."
"I am ineligible from entering the United States under the visa waiver program and did anyway. I lied to immigration. They will find out about it now."
Faith made a surprised face and shook her head.
"Why did you do such a thing?"
"It happened to be the only possible thing to do. Let's forget about it." Faith acted not convinced; she appeared digging more. "Tell me what it means please!"

Mono searched for some comforting words in his brain.
"Let's have some food honey; I am starving. Let's talk about it later." "Ok, let's start with a burrito, we are here but later at home you need to give me the whole picture because I am feeling lost now."

"Hey look, there is Gene."
Mono entered the restaurant right after Faith.
After a few steps, both arrived at Gene's table.
He quickly jumps up from his chair.
"Hey, guys. Happy to have you back in Miami Mono."
Gene, the American lawyer, had an impish smile on his face.
"Hey, Gene my partner it's good to be back here, especially after the incident this morning."
"I heard about it. I hope you let me know if I can help you out."
"I am fine for now, don't worry. It's a problem I need to deal with later." Gene doesn't seem convinced, but he decided to let it go. Faith felt abandoned.
"Hey, guys don't forget about me here. Let's hit the buffet; I'm hungry."
"That's a superb idea. I am starving as well."
"So what are the next steps?"
"Start eating a delicious dinner for example now."
"You got me Faith, let's enjoy the food first."
Mono reinitiated the conversation little later.

"We are creating the artwork for the album. We have an appointment with Cre8me, Inc. in Hollywood tomorrow."
"Do you guys already have an idea in mind?"
"We have a clear picture. We know what we want."
"Well, that's something," with a grin on his face.
"Do you have any news about an investor?"
"It's very complicating, times aren't good, but I am confident I can close with a potential one soon."
Faith jumped in. "We need to have access to new financial resources soon."
"I am on it," Gene replied.
"I trust you guys, and I am sure you have something good going."
"What are the plans for tonight?" Gene did change the subject.
"We want to meet Kelly at Ocean's Eleven and grab some drinks there."
"Sounds good to me the tab is on me guys. Let's ask for the bill and get out of here. I will see both of you tomorrow afternoon at the office, I guess."
"Yes," Faith, Mono.

The bar Ocean's Eleven it seemed to be a good place to hang out, meet some friends for cheap drinks or grab some munchies food after a late night out. Kelly appeared sitting at the bar. Kelly happened to be a hot, blonde Miami Dolphins cheerleader. Faith, Mono entered the dimly lit bar.

"I am so happy to see you guys. These dudes here are already bothering me."
"Aw, poor Kelly...but we are here to help you out now."
"It is great to see you, Blondie," Mono teased as always.
"Don't forget me here, girl!"
She gave her friend a big hug.
"I haven't seen you for such a long time. How is life to treat you these days?"
"Not so bad I have a new boyfriend, and I want to tell you all about it. Let's have a welcome drink. The first round is on me! I will order the same as always?"
"Yes, sure," Faith, Mono.

"Oh no..........I have a major headache," Faith groaned after she woke up.
Mono occurred standing with a huge smile on his face in front of her bed.
"Good morning sweetie," Mono began the morning conversation. I passed by Starbucks twenty minutes ago. I have coffee and some fresh bagels for us.
"How can you be this fresh? I remember the drinks; you drank a lot of Cuba Libre last night? Faith groaned again.
"I stayed already swimming in the pool in the morning for 30 minutes."
"Get out of here. I can stand this hyperactivity so early in the morning."

Faith surely appeared to be irritated this early in the morning.

He acted laughing at her.

"Okay, okay, breakfast will be served in 20 minutes, boss. Get ready; we only have one hour to be at Kiley's place. I will set the breakfast table on the balcony.

The couple' arrived on time to the appointment. Kiley acted as the junior boss at Cre8me, Inc., a young and trendy creative agency offering various services in Hallandale Florida.

It meant to be the first time meeting, and neither of them knew what to expect from each other. After an exchange of some kindnesses, Faith briefly explained the music project. Kiley's face turned into a huge smile.

"Guys, I don't see any problems besides maybe the time frame. Four weeks is not much time; today is Saturday. Let me come up with some ideas by next Friday.

How does it sound to you guys?"

"Mmmhmm," Mono replied. "What do you think, Faith?"

"I believe it is fine. We have time next week to do some research. We won't lose any time."

"Good, guys, we have a deal. I will send you a PayPal money request for a fifty percent advance payment," Kiley continued.

"That's fine with us. We will be back next Friday at 10 am. Is that good for you?" she asked.
"I guess 9 am would be much better," his response.
"Okay, this time is good as well," she agreed.
"What are you guys doing now? A beautiful afternoon at the pool today is waiting?" Kiley asked.
"No way," Faith said. "I wish we could, but we need to drive to our office now. Gene is already waiting."
"He works on a Saturday afternoon?" Kiley asked incredulously.
"Gene works six days a week and most holidays as well. He doesn't know what a vacation is."
Kiley nodded slowly and wrapped up the meeting with good wishes.
"I hope you guys have a lovely weekend. We will see each other next Friday."
On the way home Jam & Spoon—featuring Plavka - "Kaleidoscope Skies" appeared hitting from the car sound system.

Gene sat behind his desk looking over some documents while they both entered his office. He looked up for a second and asked them to give him a minute.
"There is some coffee waiting for you in the conference room. I will be with you shortly. I put Mono's post on the table already."
Mono checked the mail.
"Do you get anything interesting?" Faith asked.

"We need to pay our postbox, that's all."
"Oh no not now, please. I screwed up about a deadline I guess."
Mono paused as he opened up another white envelope.
"What's up?"
"My California Corporation has a reminder from the IRS. I will deal with it next week."
"Hi, guys!" Gene piped in. "How played the meeting with your design guy out?"
"We need you to draw up a short contract. Cre8me, Inc. will deliver the artwork print ready by May 15 at the latest." Faith explained.
"You guy want a work-for-hire contract?"
"Exactly," her answer.
"When do you need the contract ready?"
"Next Thursday would be good."
"That won't be a problem."
"Listen guys do you need me for anything more?" Mono asked. "I need to check my emails."
"Me too, actually," Faith jumped in.
"No problem, it's all good for now. Why don't we go for a tennis match to my club after work together?
"We want," Faith replied for both. "Please reserve a Court".

DJ Peran called Mono, opened the conversation
babbling on without giving a chance to a response.
"Hey! How are you doing? How is life in Miami? Long
time no talk."
"It's all good here. What about you?"
"I am more than good my friend. I played at the
"AHP" party at The Palace in Hollywood past
Saturday night our mix album as a DJ set, as the
headliner.
Do you want to know how people reacted?"
Mono could imagine DJ Peran's happy face this very
same moment.
"You tell me, Brother. But give me a second I want to
light a Marlboro Light cancer stick for this occasion. I
waited for this news a very long time. I want to enjoy
it."
Peran went on. "Midway - "Monkey Forest" happened
to be indeed the perfect intro. I got the crowd's
attention straight away. 4 Strings - "Into the Night"
convinced the last doubters. Connector and Acer
pushed the people. Armin van Buuren presents
Rising Stars - "Clear Blue Moon" put them literally in
heaven. Club Attack - "Solid Sleep" - Paul van Dyk -
Remix worked like doping. Acer - "The Mixmaster"
kept them on track. I began playing Rank 1 featuring
Shanokee - "Such is Life" in the middle of my set,
made the crowds jumping.

Mauro Picotto -"Ultima Hora," Chris Liebig - "Analogon" – Gaetano Remix worked all perfect. The DJ Tiesto - "Suburban Train" kept them going. Svenson & Gielen - "Twisted" gave another push to the crowds. Peran –"Good Time" made the people happy. Sonic Inc - "I feel for you" and Ralphie B - "Massive" played out as fantastic closings."
Peran went on.
"The crowd's freaking out didn't want me to leave the stage after my show."

"Peran, Peran, Peran," Mono shouted into the phone. "This is more fucking freaking cool dude than sex. Faith says hi by the way. She is sitting next to me."
"Give her a big hug."
"I will; we are still working on the cover. You should have an email about it with an update. Check." "Man you let me wait for it for a long time. Aliens I understand it correctly?"
"Yes, aliens don't need a visa." Mono had a smile on his face.
"This is great man! It is cool. That is art!"
"Wait, I will put you on speaker. Could you please repeat what you just said.......?"
"We will have a meeting with a talented local drawing artist shortly" Faith explained.
"You guys are inspiring me all of the time."

"Hahaha," Mono responded to DJ Peran's remarks. "This is our goal. The Problem occurred to be we have little to show so far."

"Guys, I can't wait to see it."

"Hold on, Peran. First, we need to find out if the artist is up for the task."

"Who is he?"

"We got very lucky. We got the contact through DJ Lex, Dawn's friend." Faith explained.

"DJ Lex? I met both at the gig in Rio de Janeiro?"

"Right," Mono answered.

"The party at the samba school I forgot the name?"

"Unidos da Tijuca," Mono answered.

"How are they?"

"They are both fine and still in love." Faith answered.

"Anyway," Mono continued. "The artist is Marco Di Porto. He lives here in Miami."

"Give me the story?" DJ Peran asked.

"You will have to wait. The story remains unfolding."

"Tell me at least the name of our album now. I have been curious since our first brainstorm session in Eric's studio ages ago." "I know my friend, I know. I am sorry about that. I appreciate your understanding and patience a lot."

"Thomas is bothering us as well about it. All are curious including us. Believe me." Faith added.

"After we have spoken with the drawing artist tomorrow afternoon, we will let you know what will happen. Is this okay with you?" Mono asked.

Peran acted waving his options and answered.

"That sounds good to me. I need to run anyway now. Please let me know. I wish you guys a nice rest of the day."

Suddenly DJ Peran ended the phone conversation.

"Haha, you confused him."
"I guess so. It seemed hard for me not to tell DJ Peran more about the artwork."
"He can live with it. He has a lot of patience with you, and he trusts your work."
"What about lunch, Faith?"
"Yeah it's an excellent Idea I guess, but our plan still worries me a lot."
"No worries. It's time for The Cheesecake Factory. It's my treat today. Let's leave now, please."
Mono acted starving.
"We will work on the marketing in the afternoon."
"No, I can't. I forgot to tell you. I will meet Heather this afternoon at the Aventura Mall."
"Haha, shopping time," he teased. "It's fine with me."
"Why don't you come with us?"
"Anthony from Quantum Entertainment will call this afternoon."
"What does he want?"
"He wants to promote our album to some trendy indie record stores around Melrose Place and in Down Town L.A. for the commission."
"He is a movie person. Does he work in music as well?"
"That's Anthony's real passion, and he is in love with our DJ list."
"Where electronic dance music crossed his ways?"

"We met at the Cannes Film Festival two years ago. Our friend Joey Horvitz appeared promoting the "Cutaway" movie release party on the Ritz Carlton beach; with DJ Peran and Steve Castro as the headliner for the night. The VIP guest list featured stars as Michael Madsen, Tom Berenger, Stephen Baldwin, Dennis Rodman, Maxine Bahns, Philip Glaser, Guy Manos, Tony Griffin, Michael Peckman, Ray from 2 Unlimited, Elisa from Ramin Project and others. Anthony happened to be an invited guest for the night."
"Does Steve Castro host his parties at The Palace in Hollywood still?"
"Yes there, Key Club, House of Blues you name it together with TJ. They are legends already. Let's leave please?"
 "Okay, but I still want to hear more about your secret Anthony plans one of these days."
"Sure, it will be my pleasure. I promise."

"Hi, Kiley!" The couple' greeted him as both entered his office.
"Good morning guys. Grab some chairs. I have something to show you."
Kiley's large office desk looked like a central command in a space ship.
"These are just some ideas for the front cover," Kiley said and pointed to a huge computer screen on the left side of his desk.

"It's something like the atmosphere combined with a lot of colors and movement. The story could start in the space and could after final on the Earth."
Kiley looked at them, looking for some signs of approval in both faces. But Kiley couldn't see any visible reaction.
"Well......I like parts of your outer space idea, but not as the origin. We see the space more as a medium of conveyance somehow. We want to display more of a deeper sense."
"Listen."
Faith demanded all attention.
"Yesterday we met with Marco Di Porto, a talented drawing artist. We explained our wish and gave him qualified information about our journey and electronic dance music in general. Marco will come up with something by Sunday evening."
Mono stepped in.
"So the question now is would you be able to edit and process his drawings digital?" Mono asked."
"I need to see the drawings first. But I am pretty sure that we will find a solution," Kiley replied. "I am getting more excited about this project."
"So are we," Faith responded.
"I have been listening to your promo CD. I checked on your guy DJ Peran as well. It's honestly the kind of music I would never have checked for at a record store, partly because it almost entirely has no airplay the U.S. radio world. It's fair to say that the music hit me instantly. I happened positively surprised. I found out that your guy hit the UK charts with his song "Good Time." Did you guys know about that?"

"Sure we do, but as an artist, Peran is with Spinnin Records in the Netherlands. So, all of the credit for that release goes to them. I love this song very much." Mono declared.

"Kiley, did you get the advance payment?" Faith asked, changing the subject of the conversation.

"Sure I did. Thank you, by the way. I would suggest that we meet on Monday afternoon for our next session. I don't want to waste any more time. Maybe we can schedule a meeting in the late afternoon,"

"Perfect. We will be here around 4 pm on Monday." She decided for both of them.

"In case something goes wrong with Marco we will let you know by email," she continued.

"Are you guys going back to your office now?" Kiley wanted to know.

"No, my sister Jennifer he is in town so that we will meet her for lunch at Katz Deli. We love that place."

"Yep we do," Mono added, smiling.

"Why you don't come with us? Join us for lunch. Jennifer is a cute girl."

Faith tried to convince Kiley.

"Okay, sure. Just give me a few seconds to clean up my mess here. I would love to join you guys. I haven't been to Katz's in ages.

"Mono....wake up honey please!"

Jam & Spoon Mix – "The Age of Love" happened to be pounding in the room. The sound slowly started to wake him up.
Faith appeared screaming and pushing his limp body'.
"Oh no! I feel like I have a dragon living in my head." He moaned.
"Haha, do you remember anything about last night?" Faith teased.
"We appeared at Club Space in Downtown right? Oh my god! This pain is killing me. I feel like shit."
"We happened to be kicked out of the club. Do you remember any of it?"
"Wait a second....the last thing I remember seemed to be that we tried to finish a huge bottle of Bacardi Gold, sitting in the VIP area with some freaky people next to us. Oh and we wet kissing Kelly together on the dance floor."
Mono smiled.
"Why did they kick us out of the club?"
"I have no idea! You went to the bathroom together with a chick. After that, a security guy approached me rudely to tell me that the stuff kicked you out of the club. Don't you remember any of that?"
"Ugh, I can't even remember leaving the club. I have no clue how we made it home."
"We didn't go back. We went straight from Space to Hollywood."
"From Downtown Miami, we drove to Hollywood? What? What did we do there?"
"We went to "The Coral Cafe" for a late breakfast."
"Oh, Faith. I am so sorry about it. Seemed it awful?"
"Don't go there," she smiled.

"I did have a lot of fun watching you all of the time. Honestly, I don't remember that much of the night either. The party will remember as a crazy night. I am just glad that we made it home safely."
"My god I feel like shit. We slept the entire fucking day."
"Whatever, don't stress too much. Get in the shower and freshen up. We are running a little late. We are supposed to meet Marco in 15 minutes.
"Is it already that late? How could I be so stupid and get so wasted? Give me 30 minutes, and please call Marco and tell him we will be late. I need a cold shower..............."
"What did Marco say?"
Mono asked Faith as he walked out of the bathroom, rubbing a clean white towel over his shaggy blonde hair.
"Don't worry; Marco is still working on our drawings. Do you want to eat a sandwich before we leave?"
"Food? Please don't mention eating right now."
"Hahaha, okay, I know how it goes with you. Take some Advil, now."
"That could help a little, but a new stomach would be a ton better."
"I heard Publix has a sale on stomachs this weekend," she teased.
"Please have some mercy with me. What do we need for the meeting?"
"Nothing but a clear head we will need for sure."
"That will be hard for me, but I will do my best, I promise."
"Oh shit!"
"What's up?"

"We don't have a car. We took a cab home last night."
"Oh, no."
"I am kidding. I acted just testing your memory."
"Whoa, you shouldn't have driven after that crazy night. We are lucky. Okay now, let's get out of here."

"Do you see him?"
"Marco might be inside the place. Let me check."
"Bring him out to the patio, please. I just can't stand the air conditioning right now," Mono asked pitifully. One minute later she came out of the restaurant through a side door connected to the patio, Marco walking in tow.
"Hi, Mono! It's good to see you. I heard you had a pretty rough time at Club Space last night."
"It seemed more kind of a morning thing, Brother happy to see you too."
Mono appeared half-smiling.
"Sit down, please. Do you want something to drink?"
"No thanks, maybe some water please."
The party animals occurred to be sitting together on one side of the table and Marco on the other.
"There stayed not so much time for me to complete the task but I came up with some inspiring ideas."

Marco opened up a folder he had hidden in his bag. Inside the folder appeared four sheets of paper. He carefully placed all on top of the table, facing the couple'. A flashback hit Mono instantly. The moment both, he and Wagges discovered "our force" at a DJ Dag live show - Dorian Gray Frankfurt 16.04.1988. Mono forgot about his headache instantly. Automatically, he reached out for his pack Marlboro light and took a cigarette.

Faith knew his habits too well. When he reached a level of total concentration, he always needed to have a cigarette between his fingers.

"Can you see it?" Mono asked.

"For me, it's a puzzle right now. But yes, I can," Faith replied.

Marco interrupted the little chat.

"This isn't a finished piece of work at all."

"I know. But still, I can totally picture our tale from the fade in until the fade out. These drawing are amazing. It's like you have been together with us all of the time." Mono said.

"These Alien dolls, they look terrific." Faith said.

"I agree. These four images express our journey entirely. I am euphoric with your work so far."

"Honestly when you guys first explained your vision to me, I had serious doubts. I didn't think that this kind of work would be possible in such a short time. You like it?"

"Give me five my man."

Faith added, "Sure we do."

"When we can have the final five drawings?" Mono asked.

"By the end of the week, I guess."

"You are kidding," she responded, exasperated.
"Why?"
Mono tried to explain it.
"We have an appointment with our graphic designer tomorrow afternoon. You have fifteen hours to complete your work. There will be no time for any more changes."
"Guys, that is impossible. I have a job tomorrow in South Beach. This job pays a lot of money, which I need badly."
"We will pay you 25 percent more," she offered.
"It's a shame or fame, Marco. We need you."
"Okay, I think, give me a second. I will do everything in my power to have the drawing ready before I leave for South Beach tomorrow morning, at around 9 am. That's the best I can offer. But how I can get the drawings to you after?"
"Take this business card. Call the courier service as soon as you finished the work. They will pick them up at any time at your place within 30 minutes, like the old Domino's Pizza only the other way around," she directed.
"Okay, guys, let's do this. I am out of here. I have a lot of work in front of me. I wish you all the best with your project. "
Both hugged Marco and said goodbye.
"Thank you. We appreciate your help."
The couple' stayed at the table to discuss further.
"Wow, this looks promising. I only hope that Kiley can work with these drawings."
"Don't worries be happy now!" he said. "He can, and I am sure he will. It's already 8.30, wow."
"What should we do with this early Sunday evening?"

"Do you have something on your mind?"
"I guess I do……..," she said, touching his little booty.

Gene called Faith cell phone.
"Hi Faith good morning it's all good today?"
"Hi, Gene good morning it's all fantastic."
"I just now accepted a package delivered."
"That's great news!"
"What is it?" Gene asked.
"These are Marco's drawings for our project artwork. We met the guy yesterday evening. He did an excellent job."
"May I open it?"
"Sure, go ahead."
"Where are you guys?"
"We are checking out some companies in South Beach."
"Any luck so far?"
"We have a few decent options, but we keep searching for a better deal. Hey, we will be by the office around lunch. Let's talk about it later." Mono yelled a greeting in the background.
"Thank you. Okay, see you guys later. By the way, I have more surprises waiting for you guys."
"Oh, really you have?"
Faith seemed too distracted to ask for details.
"I need to run, goodbye for now."
Everything is okay for us?" Mono asked.

"Yes, it's all fine. We already got the package from Marco. I am so curious to see his final work.
I feel much better now. Also, Gene talked about other surprises he has for us."
"Sounds nice I love good surprises. Marco's work is a milestone for our project."
She interrupted his mental travels with a dose of reality, as always.
"Still we have a lot of blank fields."
"Look, there is a Starbucks. Let's grab a coffee and sit down for a while. I want to compare the offers from these companies before we drive back to the office."
"You are a real Starbucks addict. What about Taco Bell instead? It's lunchtime already.
"It's too crowded there at this time of the day. I don't need food right now. Are you hungry?"
"I guess a Muffin will do it for me its Starbucks ok."

Mono analyzed one of the proposals. Faith appeared busy on her laptop. "Do you have a minute?" Mono asked. "Sure, what's up?"
"We just cannot afford these South Beach companies. These estimates are ridiculously high. We need more time to search a better deal, a place we can print the posters and fliers affordable. We need to be flexible."
"What are you suggesting?"
Mono seemed not ready for an answer and kept thinking.

"I believe we should concentrate on the label for now. It's important that MBBs partner can start printing the album in Brazil; our release date is already in danger. I suggest we let print CD cover, booklet and back cover with the poster and fliers together all here in Miami, shipping the artwork - FedEx after to MBB in Sao Paulo."
"Do we have all of the requirements for Brazil?"
"Yes, we do. We need to convert our artwork to film."
"Mono, this is obviously the right way to go."
"I am glad you think the same way as I do," Mono smiled.
"What about your numbers?"
"I'm sorry. I am not there yet. I had many changes in the last months, and there are still too many blank fields on my sheet. I will need some time to present the entire plan to you.
Our store numbers are growing. We have Cisco for whole Japan. Through Galgano Records, we have Transworld Entertainment Corp for a chunk of major stores.
We have Hardware World Production for the indie stores.
We have FLL for Florida east coast, Uncle Sam's Music in Miami for our U.S. presentation and ReseachMusic.com for streaming the album on the Internet next year.
It is more than we could have dreamed of in the first place. In a case, we pull this off."
"It's fine, don't worry. Let's drive up to the office. I am antsy to see Marco's work."

She drove her car into the parking lot at 1550 NE Miami Gardens Drive.
Jam & Spoon–featuring Plavka - "Angel" played softly from the car sound system.
Gene appeared to drive out of the parking lot at the same moment. Gene duplicates a creature of habit, and he left his office every day, at the same time, for his lunch at his house, no matter what. You could set a clock by it.
They faced each other through the opened car windows.
"I will leave for lunch now. I put your envelope on the secretary's desk."
"Did you have a chance to have a look at Marco's drawings?" Faith asked Gene.
I happened to be too busy this morning, and I forgot about it. I am a lawyer, and I don't understand these kinds of things anyway. More importantly, Vanessa faxed back the contract signed, and I had a chat with Harold this morning. We can pick up a check at his house whenever we have time during the week.
Harold isn't even asking for any interests payments. Anyway, I will leave now, but I will be back later. Bye Guys."
"Thank you for an excellent good job. Have a nice lunch. Bye Gene."
Faith looked over to the passenger's seat.
"Did you hear what he just said?"
"I sure did. Give me five!"
"We are rich!"
"We will need any penny of it."

"I am just kidding," Faith teased. "Let's transfer the money from Bank of America later to MBB. These are huge steps in the right direction. The money ensures that we can go a long way if everything goes by plan."
"This is true, but never anything goes by plan. Gene did a great job. Do you think we should get out of the car now? It's hot!"
Faith acted laughing. "Let's do it."
The office seemed abandoned when both entered the reception area.
"Why don't we take the drawings and head to the pool at our place for the next two hours?" she offered. "I anyway can't concentrate on work right now."
"Great idea we have an exhausting evening ahead of us. Grab the envelope while I just check my emails for a second."
He re-entered the reception area a few minutes later while she appeared still staring carefully at the drawings.
"It's all in?"
"Here," she presented the drawings to him. "Have a look yourself."
She handed the sheets over to him.
Mono doesn't say a word until they reached her condo at 600 Three Islands Blvd in Hallandale.
Judging by the expression on his face, he remained in a deep trance.
He kept checking the drawings over and over again.
Jam & Spoon – "Stella" continued hitting from the car sound system.
"We are home everything okay with you?"
She interrupted his trance-like state and parked the car right in the front of the large driveway.

"I am fine, honey. Marco's drawings are copies from our minds. I am stunned."
"I know you are. I had the very same feeling."

Kiley emerged sitting in front of his central space command when they entered the office room.
Kiley opened the conversation.
You guys don't look like nerds. You guys looking like you just got back from a nice long vacation.
"That's a bit of an exaggeration, Kiley."
Faith playfully defended the 2 hours break at the pool.
"I am kidding," Kiley said.
"I like called being a nerd. My friends would call me a lot but never a Nerd," Mono laughed.
"Moving on," Kiley continued, "let me see what you have for me.
Mono handed him over the envelope with Marco's drawings. Kiley carefully placed all five in front of him on the desk. None of them spoke a single word. Kiley disrupted the silence. It is nice stuff. I should have no problem moving forward with this material. Should we start with the cover?"
"We need the label for the CD first," Mono explained "Which drawings do you guys want to use as the eye catcher?"
Faith pointed with her right hand to three of the arts on Kiley's desk.

"First, I will scan all of the drawings, which will take a while. After I need to convert the RAW image file..."
"Don't even go there, Kiley. No programmer talk. Please, just focus on what we can understand," she complained.
"Haha, okay. What about the logos?"
Mono handed over a CD-R to Kiley.
"Everything you need is on this CD."
Kiley got straight down to work.
"Let's get going on the fonts for the title."
After one hour of work, they finally came to an agreement on a font and a style.
"I understand exactly what you guys need. It will take a couple of hours of work for me. I need to minimize the size of the image to use as a label. These Aliens are dancing, right?" Kiley asked.
""Rhythm is a Dancer**" my friend," Mono answered.
"We need to decide on the color of the water."
"That's easy. Make it kind of brownish-green.
"Okay, check this out."
"Add a little more light in the center."
Faith added, "It needs to reflect the light from the arriving space ship."
"Sure, let me see what I can do. What are they carrying on that ship, by the way?"
Kiley hoped for some explanation to use for additional inspiration.
"Carrying nothing," Mono answered coyly.
"Why the ship is visiting Amsterdam?" Kiley asked more bluntly.
Faith answered this time.
"The ship is picking up both aliens, carrying the clone of "our plant.""

"So.... the aliens travel back to space?"
Kiley sounded surprised.
"The aliens are departing to new destinations."
Kiley acted shaking the head and laughing. "Guys, which plant? These are fantasies."
"Realities are born from visions my friend. We are creating reality as we speak." Mono grinned in Kiley's face.
"Where in Amsterdam is this area supposed to be?" Kiley asked.
Mono......
"It is a part of Amstelstraat by the Amstel River close to the Rembrandt Square.
"Why did you guys show this particular place on the album cover?"
"Is that part of the city where the aliens departed Amsterdam," Faith added.
"That's interesting. There are other alien's in the city?"
Kiley's questions happened less than serious.
Mono answered with a telling smile on his face.
"Our aliens have left my friend."
Kiley's face appeared wrinkled in disbelief, as he thought to himself, "these guys are pushing this thing far."
DJ Taucher – "Fantasy" - Club Mix 1 played to hit in the creative office.
Out loud, Kiley said "I suggest we take a break at this point. There isn't anything for you guys to do right now and I don't have any questions. I will put everything together, and we can meet on Thursday morning. I do have one question right now. Do I know all of the technical requirements?"

"I emailed all the info to you yesterday afternoon."
"Ah, I forgot. I already saw the mail! Okay, I will see you guys on Thursday."
"Don't get up; we can find our way out. Thank you."
"Good night," Faith kindly.
"Bye Bro," Mono said.

Just two minutes later in the car driving.
Mauro Picotto - "Ultimo Hora Ibiza" - Amsterdamcing Mix kept going from the car sound system.
"Are you happy?"
"I am and convinced that we can pull this shit off now. I am glad because we are together at this particular moment. But I am sad because I know paradise never last forever. It can be over in any given minute. What about you?"
"Think about it. It seems to me you have a fair chance to keep your insane pledge to your friend Wagges for the first time. I am happy. Should we call Thomas in Sao Paulo to give him the news? What do you think?"
Mono checked the watch and opened his agenda.
Massive – Ralphie – Amsterdamcing Mix occurred hitting.
"It's too early he is at countryside without an internet connection until tomorrow. But we could call DJ Peran. On the other hand, I don't think that's fair to Thomas. We should schedule a conference call with both of them tomorrow afternoon."

"It will be hard to get both of them on the line at the same time. You know that. DJ Peran always has a weird schedule in L.A. I will write an email to both of them. This way, we can be sure that everyone gets the correct info. Both can always email or call back tomorrow if they have any additional questions."
"I agree, let's do it after we are home."
"I have a question or two." "Go ahead."
"Which albums had the biggest impact on you in your trance life?"
"Without a doubt our 24/7 sound from ten years ago. Dane 2 Trance -"Moon Spirits" and Jam & Spoon - "Tripomanic Fairytales 2001" both blow me away. Hero's for a lot of people, me including. I like others as well of course."
"And as trance compilations of all times are concerned?"
"Ha ha, all times? The world has so many great playlists to offer. A lot of trance DJ-sets recorded on music cassette tapes are marvelous. The discotheque - "Extreme" - Trance Edition from Belgium inspired me. I like "DJ Convention – Herbststurm" both CDs a lot. The "Hot Weekend Amsterdam" records set me in a happy mood always."

"I have an answer from Thomas. MBB will pay the advance payment for the last missing license today." Faith appeared smiling, kept going.

"Thomas asked the labels and publishers to acknowledge the change of the name of the album. And here comes the bug shit. We need to change our planned release date. Brazil has enormous power problems, and companies work below capacity to save energy, the measure will continue the coming months. Why didn't he put you on cc, Mono?"
She appeared yelling from her part of the office.
"It's easy because you are in charge of the project."
All of a sudden, he stood inside Faith's office door frame.
"You know what a change of date means for us?"
"The album will arrive in Miami after we leave for Germany?"
"It means the whole project seems in danger."
"We could reschedule the date to later."
"Assuming I won't have any problem at immigration again?"
"We will plan the worst case scenario. I could handle the work alone in the beginning."
"We need to be together when our aliens arrive it works this way only."
"I know that well."
"Trust in "our force" something will come up," Faith added very convincingly.
"Did Thomas mention anything about Club Sounds?"
"Not at all why are you asking?"
"Because last time we spoke, he told me that he wants to release the album on his sub-label."
"Does it make any difference?"
"Not at all, but I guess it's a smart move. What else did Thomas write?"

"He is having problems finalizing a deal with Intergroove Brazil. He wants you to talk to them because you know the founder."
"I forwarded the mail to you already."
"What else?"
"DJ Peran's tour has been confirmed. He will have several radio show appearances in Sao Paulo. Some DJ gigs are confirmed as well."
"Did Thomas mention names?"
"Radio "Jovem Pan." Clubs span from Manga Rosa in Sao Paulo and Target Guaruja to Ibiza in Camboriu. This list remains still open."
"This is huge! Good news for the fans."
"Who made all of this happen down there?"
"Thomas and Adriana of course and you remember Yashin, right?"
"Of course I remember the guy well."
"Yashin made contact to Goncalo Vinha, Alessandro, and Persio from Nude Management. Goncalo is a key figure in the Sao Paulo electronic music scene. He is also a huge fan of progressive trance and DJ Peran. He is a producer himself."
"All did an outstanding job. It seems like we are set in Brazil, right?
"It's scary, isn't it? It's a market with endless opportunities."
"It is future talk for now."
"Will you answer Thomas's mail?"
"I have it already done check your email now."
"What do we do about DJ Peran?"
"I will tell him the news."
"Has he answered your email from last night?"
"Not yet."

"Anyway, I want to wait until he has digested the news from last night. Otherwise, he will bomb me with questions the whole day."
"Haha yes, that's our DJ Peran indeed."
"Anyway, Peran will be triumphal to hear all of it. I am a little worried about the owner from Intergroove Brazil, by the way."
"This is the company that bought the Inversus Records vinyl's from us. Intergroove Brasil acted happy at the time with that deal, if I remember correctly."
"Sure they seemed great with the deal. It's just a feeling very disturbing I have."
"Describe it better to me I want to understand it."
 "These Intergroove guys are electronic dance music pioneers in Sao Paulo. The company owner invited me to Brazil a few years ago and connected me with Thomas in the first place. I can't help it, but I feel negative forces are at play as well here. I will talk to the man, though. How are Sandy and Inversus Records doing?"
"He is doing extremely well. I will give him a call soon. We should hang out at his place one of these days."
"That's a good idea. I would like to see Sandy again soon."

Kiley greeted the couple' with a warm smile again. The lovers' reacted the same way.

"Guys come in and have a seat. It's good to see you again. I already almost finished the label and the cover.
"Hey Kiley," they both responded.
"Look at it. I changed the color of the sky a little. It looks epic now. Check it," Kiley continued pointing to the computer screen.
"Indeed," Mono nodded.
"I agree."
"But why does it have to be more epic looking in the first place? I thought it's about dancing, love, and happiness."
Kiley continued pushing both.
"It's a spectacular event, we need epic," Mono explained.
"That makes sense. It lasted a little tricky for me to get it done. Check it out."
"It's cool Kiley; I love it."
"The label looks awesome," Faith piped in.
"The title, logos, the copyright info, printing company info and the numbers it's all there. I agree."
"Check the cover. I have the file open on this screen." Kiley appeared pointing to another huge flat screen on his desk and asked Mono.
"What more information do you guys want to include on the cover?"
"We want the title and the Stars placed, of course."
"Okay, give me the names."

 ""Amsterdamcing - A Story of Trance Music," mixed by DJ Peran–featuring songs from DJ Tiesto, 4 Strings, Rank 1 Feat Shanokee, Chris Liebing, Sonic Inc, Acer, Armin van Buuren - presents Rising Star, Mauro Picotto, and Solid Sleep - Paul van Dyk Remix."
"We are running out of space."
"Just write, 'and more....'"
"That could work. Give me one second. Okay, what you guys think?"
Both focused on the image on Kiley's screen.
Mono acted not convinced.
"Will we lose impression?"
"What do you mean?"
"I am talking about the colors."
"I guess the print will be a bit lighter. We will conduct a test print anyway. But we shouldn't be worrying about that just yet," Kiley pushed forward.
"First let's talk about the inside booklet. Which background color do you want?"
Kiley looked with a question mark face at Faith.
"I think we should go with the same colors but just a little lighter in the center. We want to show an alien's encounter, the moment both initiate the cloning of "our plant.""
"How do they do that?"
"Ayla-Ayla" – DJ Taucher-Remix continued beating from Kiley's stereo sound system. The group with nodding heads to the beats.

"You see these tiny yellow lights on all hands? They use them to communicate and interact with "our plant." The aliens transmit magic words through these, and, in response, she breeds a clone and activates the movement of the clone directly towards the aliens. Both aliens are tightly connected to each other through the right hands during the whole transfer."
"Why do they need to be connected?" Kiley asked.
"An unbelievable amount of energy is transmitted and absorbed. Only a couple together can process and host it after. The two are imperative."
"It needs to be a female and male together?" Kiley appeared shaking his head.
"It could be two male aliens or two female aliens; sex doesn't matter. What is important is that the couple' appeared mentally united."
"Do the aliens only communicate with the plant?" Kiley emerged curiously.
"They communicate with each other telepathically and with others trough different channels." Faith explained, with a smile on her face.
"Why they are wearing those eyeglasses?" Kiley asked Mono.
"Apparently the eyeglasses are a natural part of their heads and connected with their minds. These glasses are very sophisticated and powerful. It enables them to send individual messages directly to human brains."
Kiley acted laughing the ass off. "Why are they doing that?"

"Those encoded messages systematically alter brain functions. It permanently expands the horizons of the receiving mind." Now Mono appeared smiling.
"It has an immediate effect on the brain just like drugs have?"
"It's a long term but steady process." Faith answered.
"What about the flashing light on both stomachs?"
"The clone continues broadcasting codes permanently, received by altered human brains."
Kiley's shook his head, "Come on, guys, what both are sending at this moment?"
"It's all about our DJs," Mono answered dryly.
"So.... Should I create speech bubbles coming out of the hands?
"Yes, from the left of the male alien."
"What is the male alien saying?"
Faith reached into her briefcase and took out a piece of paper and handed it over to Kiley, "This is the magic formula. Use this letters, please."
"You guys are kidding me. I can't read it."
Faith tried to comfort Kiley.
"Check my last email to you it's all there. Just copy and paste the text."
"What is written on this note?"
"Haha...Calm down Kiley," Mono teased.
Kiley appeared on fire.
"I will figure it out eventually," He responded.
"You absolutely will, although it isn't all that easy. That said; let's get back to the task at hand."
"I am sorry, guys. I promised my dad I would help him out with some work today. We are having some server problems. I will finish the rest of the job later today. Tomorrow we can work on your back cover."

Faith kept pushing Kiley a bit more.
"We need the files for the label today."
"Give me few minutes. I will burn a CD-R for you."
"Let's meet tomorrow morning right after breakfast. I will discover your alien secrets overnight."
Both quickly laughed at Kiley's remarks.
"Don't worry. Thanks for the work and we will see you tomorrow....."

"Hahaha, that played out so funny. Did you see Kiley's face when I gave him the piece of paper when he saw the letter fonts?" Faith asked.
"I sure did. It's great that we piqued Kiley's interest with it. I like working with him."
"Me too, Kiley is a young, bold and talented guy. Shall I drive to my mom's place? We could pick her up for a late lunch."
"Let's first decide on the files."
"You are right. Let's drive to the office. We will drop the CD and schedule a pick-up with Convert Film?"
"Yes, it's easier than us driving up there."
"It will be another ten days until our files make it to Thomas's record printing company in the Amazon. Thirty days more to process and print the album."
"That's okay - we are on track. In 40 days, the records land in Sao Paulo; our aliens will arrive even earlier. Thomas and Adriana will take care of it all. I am concerned about Miami."
"I am born here don't worry."

Madagascar - "Art of Trance" - Cygnus X Remix kept going from the car sound system.

Faith and Mono appeared happy when both left the office building.
"Let's drive down to Coral Gables." Faith suggested.
"Baja Fresh?"
"As always, you can read my mind. We could make the patio our office for the afternoon. Maybe we can also take a little walk in downtown Coral Gables afterward."
"You have already convinced me."
"Interesting fact, Coral Gables was one of the first planned communities in the United States. It is the home of the University of Miami. Did you know that?"
"Now I know. I like the Mediterranean Revival style of the district. But to be honest, right now I am thinking more about Burrito Mexicano, charbroiled chicken, simmered black beans and chopped cilantro.
"Haha, you made me hungry. I am going to go for a Diablo Shrimp Burrito today."
"That sounds excellent as well."
"This was soooooo good........"
"Yeah, but I am tired now."
"Yeah me too, kinda. And it's too crowded here. We can't work here today. Do you have any other ideas?"

"We could walk a little to digest our food after we can drive a few blocks to Sunrise Harbour. It is close to Coconut Grove. Do you remember that little coffee place?"
"Your friend Michelle lives in the neighborhood there, right?"
"More or less, yeah honey."
"I remember a little restaurant there only. But I believe it's an interesting idea. Let's walk first after we see. Tell me a little about Coral Gables downtown history."
Mono enjoyed having her as a tour guide in Miami.
"Well," she began, "the Coral Gables downtown commercial district emerged designed to be only four blocks wide and two miles long. The developer for the entire Coral Gables appeared to be George Edgar Merrick.......................... ***".

Mono and Faith entered Kiley's creative place carrying huge smiles. Kiley is suddenly getting up from his chair to greet the couple'.
"I have deciphered the alien formula, hehe."
"Good morning!" both greeted Kiley.
"Welcome to our secret society. What is the male alien transmitting, Kiley?" Faith asked.
"It is evident. Don't you think so?"
"Don't try to confuse me, Mono. Anyway, I figured out the magic words, 'our trance mission is complete.' What do you think about that, guys?"

Kiley appeared smirking with a twinkle in his eyes; it seemed forever before he began talking again.
"Did I pass the test?"
"You passed this test! How did you figure it out?" Faith asked.
"I checked all of the font styles I had available and compared the letter types. I found the "Rosetta Stone" software, essentially. I still can't figure out what the female alien continues communicating. I have only an idea thus far. Is she synced with the male alien's mind, isn't she?"
"Interesting........." Mono trailed off. "I believe Kiley can communicate with the aliens already. What do you think?"
"I say we have a lot more work to do here." Faith commented.
"I still have a lot of questions about your mysterious force, but I promised you guys we would work on the back cover. I have some questions first."
"The female alien lifts the male alien up to the spaceship....why she seems leading?" "The female alien rescues the male alien while he transmits a message to "our force" asking for immediate support."
Mono bounced in.
"As the transfer of the clone nears conclusion, the hidden forces keep trying to separate the male alien from the female alien, to disrupt the signal, to stop the process and capture the clone."
"I prepared something nice for the background. What do you guys think?"
"Let's give it a shot. It looks good," Mono said.

"What other content do we need to include on the back cover? I want to try a few different designs first hold on a second."
Mono and Faith waited in patience for a while.
"Track list, logos, company contact, website, copyright info, all of the credits and the barcode. Just confirm with our list," Faith said.
Kiley acted busy for quite a time, playing around with various layouts until all finally came to an agreement.
Crazy Malamute - "A Good And Decent Man?" emerged going in the office.

Kiley placed the images of the arts on different screens.
Faith interrupted in the middle of his work.
"Hold on! Please zoom out on the hand of the male alien, but do it slowly. Now zoom in. Do the same with both heads. Both bodies together now.
How do you feel about it, Mono?"
Both stared intensely at the inside cover for what seemed like forever.
"Make a PowerPoint of all of the pages, starting with the cover, please....... and run it," Mono asked Kiley.
Mono stared into Faith's eyes. Faith returned the intense gaze into Mono's eyes. The moments passed, just the trance beats filled the room.
"Please print all the sheets out now," Mono asked excitedly.

Mono's and Faith's faces appeared lit up with smiles. Kiley stood up and walked over to the printer to check out the prints. All of a sudden, he jumped up and down like a kid in preschool who acted desperately to be the first to answer a teacher's question.
Faith and Mono seemed astonished but smiling.
"Guys, Hahaha, I get it. I get it all. Your Aliens just landed in America. Didn't they?"
Faith and Mono both asked the same question, at the same time. "You think so?"
DJ Peran's "Good Time" – Amsterdamcing Mix began - hitting in the room.

The End

Sources
*Unknown
**Snap
***Wikipedia
****Sven Väth /OFF

#EDM Publications
edmpub.com

Coming Soon! Coming Soon!

"The shaping of our force," check out the news! Mono appeared suggesting.

The shaping of our force (excerpt)
A story of trance music.

Michael Peckmann & Rebecca Rosen

2002 - 2006

I

Coming Home

DJ Rush & Dr. Motte - Love Parade appeared to be animating the crowds. Faith and Mono dancing together with millions of other fans from various countries around the world, in close range to the Siegessäule at the heart of the event, seeking to get all of the vibe first hand. The mission seemed to be easy to understand. 'Love, Love, Love!'
The next noon, six hours later than planned, the couple' emerged again overnighted but happy leaving Berlin. A music tape cassette by Blank & Jones — Love Parade 2000 happened to be pounding in the car.
At the state border from Potsdam to Sachsen-Anhalt, the German Customs had established a roadblock. Mono slowed down the car to 5 Km per hour expecting to pass through the hurdle quickly.

#EDM Publications
edmpub.com

The Authors

Michael Peckmann:

Michael was born in Magdeburg, East Germany. He is a truth-seeking activist inspired by the life story of Herman Hesse. Michael's political activism caught up with him early and, at 22, he was convicted of treason. He served 30 months in prison and was subsequently banned from his country. He has been traveling the world ever since.

Dr. Rebecca Rosen:

Rebecca is a neuroscientist and adventurer from Miami, Florida. She has a passion for making the complicated simple, and for bringing different groups of people together for a common cause. In between research stints, she embarked on a South American road trip filled with new stories and intriguing people. Rebecca currently lives and works in Brooklyn, New York.

#EDM Publications
edmpub.com

#EDM Publications
edmpub.com